The attorney's gaze moved slowly over her, from head to toe

"You're Zoe McInnes?" His deep voice sounded almost accusing.

"Of course I am." Zoe swept her hand around the empty cell block. "There's no one else back here, is there?"

"You want to tell me what happened with Wallace?"

"I'll tell you whatever you want. Just get me out of here."

"Why would I want to do that?"

Zoe stared at him. "Because that's your job! Helen sent you over, didn't she?"

"Helen who?"

Zoe's stomach lurched. "You're not an attorney."

"I am, but I don't know anyone named Helen."

Zoe took a deep breath, then really looked at the man. He seemed vaguely familiar, but she couldn't place him. "Who are you?"

He studied her for a moment longer. Finally he said, "I'm Gideon Tate. Wallace's other son." His hand clenched on his briefcase. "The one you didn't kill."

Dear Reader,

Years ago on a trip to the beach I saw three girls, identical triplets, along with their younger sister, who looked just like the older girls. All four of them were dressed in identical outfits. I watched those children for a long time, wondering how they felt about being triplets. About looking exactly alike, being dressed exactly alike. Did they like being one of several, being the same? Or did they yearn to be individuals, to have a separate identity? And what about their younger sister? She was like her sisters, but different. Did she feel left out, not quite as special as the other three? Those questions have lingered in my mind ever since, and they helped spark my idea for a story about triplet sisters.

I loved getting to know the eldest McInnes triplet, Zoe, and writing her story. I enjoyed how she was different, and also the same, as her two sisters. And I loved throwing her together with Gideon Tate, absolutely the last man she should ever get involved with.

I hope you enjoy reading about Zoe and Gideon. Zoe's sister Bree's story will be out in December, 2008, and Fiona's in 2009.

Margaret Watson

A PLACE
CALLED HOME
Margaret Watson

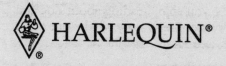

HARLEQUIN®

TORONTO • NEW YORK • LONDON
AMSTERDAM • PARIS • SYDNEY • HAMBURG
STOCKHOLM • ATHENS • TOKYO • MILAN • MADRID
PRAGUE • WARSAW • BUDAPEST • AUCKLAND

ISBN-13: 978-0-373-71508-4
ISBN-10: 0-373-71508-0

A PLACE CALLED HOME

ABOUT THE AUTHOR

Margaret Watson has always made up stories in her head. When she started actually writing them down, she realized she'd found exactly what she wanted to do with the rest of her life. Almost twenty years after staring at that first blank page, she's an award-winning, two-time RITA® Award finalist who has written twenty books for Silhouette and Harlequin Books.

When she's not writing or spending time with her family, she practices veterinary medicine. She loves everything about her job, other than the "Hey, Dr. Watson, where's Sherlock?" jokes, which she's heard way too many times. She loves pets, but writing is her passion. And that's just elementary, my dear readers.

Margaret lives in a Chicago suburb with her husband and three daughters and a menagerie of pets.

Books by Margaret Watson

HARLEQUIN SUPERROMANCE

For my brother John, a hero in so many ways.

PROLOGUE

"ZOE, IF YOUR MOTHER and I got divorced, which one of us would you stay with?"

Eleven-year-old Zoe stared out the windshield of the car, her stomach in a knot. "I don't want to choose," she said softly.

"What if you had to?"

"Are you and Mom getting a divorce?"

"Of course not. Your mother would never leave me. She adores me. Just like you and your sisters." Zoe could feel him looking at her. "Right?"

"Yes, Daddy." Zoe knew what she was expected to say.

"So would you stay with me?" He tugged lightly at her ponytail and she twitched away from him, her long swath of dark hair brushing her cheek.

"You said you're not getting divorced."

"Just pretend," he said impatiently.

"I'd stay with my sisters," Zoe said, sneaking a glance at her father. He wouldn't like that answer. "Triplets stay together."

"That wasn't what I asked," he said, his voice rising.

The smell of his pipe tobacco was making Zoe feel sick to her stomach. *Please get home soon.*

"I'll ask your sisters. They'd stay with me."

"Then Mom would be lonely."

"That would be her punishment for leaving me."

"You said she'd never leave you," Zoe mumbled.

"You're defiant today." Anger filled her father's voice. "I don't like defiant girls. Your sisters aren't defiant."

Zoe knew how Bree and Fiona would answer their father's question. Bree would tell him she'd stay with him. Fiona would choose their mother. Fee never cared when he started yelling. She just got that look in her eyes like she was far away.

Zoe's stomach churned until she was afraid she'd puke all over the car. Then he'd really be mad.

"You'd stay with me, wouldn't you, Zo?" He used his convincing voice, the one he used when he wanted her to agree with him. "Don't you love me?"

"I love you, Daddy," she said dutifully.

"Then why wouldn't you stay with me?"

The car slowed as they approached their driveway. It had barely stopped before Zoe jumped out and dashed into the backyard. A tangle of tall honeysuckle bushes crowded against the fence, and she crawled beneath them.

She sat there until she was sure he hadn't followed her. Then she slumped against the fence, inhaling the sweet scent of the honeysuckle blossoms, and let the tears roll down her face.

Eighteen years later

STALE AIR ENVELOPED Zoe as she opened the door to the house and stepped inside. Her sister Bree followed more slowly, her son trailing behind. Twelve-year-old Charlie, full of preteen attitude, scowled as he scuffled across the threshold. Bree took two steps, then stopped as she gazed around the foyer.

"It hasn't changed at all." Bree touched the marble-topped table below the gilt-framed mirror, smoothing her finger over the white surface.

"Home, sweet home," Zoe said. She switched on the hall light to banish the shadows. "Are you sure you'll be okay here? You're welcome to stay at my house."

"We'll be fine here, Zoe," Bree said as she stepped into the living room. The picture of their father, wearing the gown he donned for Collier College graduations, still dominated the wall over the fireplace. Snapshots of their mother with the three girls, his triplets, stood on an end table tucked into a corner.

"Better you than me," Zoe muttered.

"Is there even a television in this friggin' museum?" Charlie asked, kicking at the front door.

"Charlie McInnes!" Bree rounded on her son. "Do you want to eat a bar of soap?"

Charlie rolled his eyes behind his glasses. "Sorry, Mom. Is there a television in this *house?*"

"There is," Zoe said. Poor Charlie. She wouldn't be looking forward to spending the next few months in this sad, haunted place, either. It hadn't felt welcoming since her mother died seventeen years ago. "I'll bring over the video game console from my house, all right?"

"Okay," Charlie said. He looked a little more cheerful.

"It's going to take a long time to go through everything," Bree said doubtfully. She glanced at Zoe. "Unless you've already started?"

Zoe shook her head. "No, Bree, I haven't. We agreed we'd do it together. I thought we could each do our own bedroom and we'd do the rest of the house together. I can figure out what to do with the furniture. Maybe you can sort out the books and the stuff in Dad's office? Fiona's into gardening—we'll have her make the yard look good before we put the place up for sale."

"Still telling us what to do, Zo?"

"You're welcome to come up with a different plan," Zoe answered carefully. She didn't want to get into a fight on Bree's first day in town.

"No, yours makes sense," Bree answered.

"When Fiona gets here tomorrow, we'll decide what to tackle first."

Bree sank onto the staircase in the hall. "I can't believe you got her to agree to come back to Spruce Lake."

"Why wouldn't she? She has an equal say in what we do with the house. An equal responsibility, too." It hadn't been easy to persuade Fiona to come home. Their sister, her identical twin and the third triplet, had very reluctantly returned for their father's funeral six months earlier. She'd flown in and out the same day.

Bree flashed a smile. "I wish I'd been a fly on the wall during that conversation."

Bree's smile looked stiff, as if she wasn't used to smiling much, and Zoe's heart ached for her. But instead of hugging her, she gave Bree a lazy grin. "My powers of persuasion are legendary."

Bree snorted. "Yeah, you got me to come back here and live in this house full of nightmares. I'm still not sure how you did that."

They both knew why Bree had come back—she had no other options. But Zoe said lightly, "Trade secret." She pushed away from the wall. "Let me help you carry your stuff upstairs." She glanced at her nephew, who stood with his hands in the pockets of his baggy jeans as he studied the living room. "Charlie, why don't you stay in my old room? The southern exposure will be warmer for your reptiles. Is that okay?"

Charlie brightened. "That's great, Aunt Zo. Thanks."

ZOE AND BREE were sorting haphazardly through the clothes in their father's closet the next morning when they heard a car door slam in the driveway. By the time they opened the front door, Fiona was standing at the bottom of the steps, staring at the house. When she saw them, she took a deep breath, squared her shoulders and said, "I'm here."

"Hey, Fee," Zoe said, running down to hug her, Bree following. Fiona smelled like a mysterious foreign flower, and her face, although identical to Zoe's, looked exotic and striking. Way too glamorous for a small Wisconsin college town.

Fiona hugged her back, then embraced Bree, who said, "I love the hair, punk."

Fiona touched her short, spiky black hair that was tipped with magenta. "Yeah?"

Bree winked. "Spruce Lake-ans are going to love it, too."

"Don't pay any attention to her," Zoe said, linking an arm through Fiona's. "I've seen plenty of kids in town with even wilder hair."

Fiona finally smiled. "That makes me feel a whole lot better, Zo."

"Come on in," Zoe said, coaxing her toward the house. She could feel Fiona tense as they got closer to the door. "Hey, Charlie," she called. "Your aunt Fiona is here."

Charlie clattered down the stairs. "Hi, Aunt Fee." His eyes widened. "Sweet hair."

"Hi, Charlie." Fiona relaxed a little as she hugged him.

Bree pulled her gangly son aside. "Go get your aunt's things from the car."

Charlie brushed past them as they stepped into the foyer of the house, and Fiona's eyes traveled over the faded couch and dusty end tables. "Nothing's changed," she said in a flat voice.

"Not yet." Zoe drew Fiona toward the kitchen. "Come have some lemonade and we can catch up."

The front door banged as they headed down the dark, narrow hall. "Is this all you have, Aunt Fee?"

Zoe turned around to see Charlie holding one small carry-on. Fiona didn't bother to look. "Yeah, that's it."

Bree exchanged glances with Zoe. "Not staying long, Fee?"

"I have stuff to do back in the city," Fiona answered, not meeting her eyes.

Zoe had no trouble reading Bree's expression. Years had passed since they'd left home, but nothing much had changed with the McInnes triplets.

None of them wanted to be in this house.

All of them were trying to figure out how to leave.

CHAPTER ONE

THE DOOR OF Joe's Coffee House crashed open, startling Zoe as she took a sip from the paper cup. Her hand jerked and coffee spilled on her messenger bag.

"Darn it," she muttered, grabbing a handful of napkins from the stack on the counter.

"Zoe. I've been looking for you."

The voice was low and threatening, and Zoe spotted Wallace Tate in the doorway, his face a mottled red.

"Wallace." She shifted, bracing herself against the counter behind her. "What can I do for you?"

"You know just fine what you can do for me." He walked toward her, his hands clenched into fists. "You tell Sally you were wrong. You hear me?"

The three customers waiting for their coffee froze, and the people sitting at the tables glanced up from their laptops and their newspapers. The only sound was the hiss of the espresso machine. Zoe ignored everyone except Wallace. "Why would I do that? I wasn't wrong, and we both know it."

Wallace leaned closer, his thin lips compressed and his faded blue eyes filled with rage. He smelled musty and old. "So help me God, you're going to be sorry you crossed me."

"What are you going to do to me, Wallace? Send me to jail?" Zoe smiled. "Been there, done that."

She heard a quick intake of breath from another customer.

"You never were smart enough to back off, were you?" He raised his fist. "You're interfering in my personal life. I don't allow anyone to do that."

She glanced at his fist. "You want to hit me? Go ahead." Her gaze bored into his. "You'll have lots of witnesses. Or don't you hit women in front of other people?"

Wallace shoved his finger in her face. "I'm going to say this one more time, Zoe. You tell Sally you were mistaken. Or you'll regret it."

Zoe grabbed his finger. "Don't point at me." She'd been trying to keep her composure, telling herself that Wallace Tate was a pathetic old man. But now her anger sparked. "Get out of here, Wallace." She shoved his hand away from her face.

The older man stumbled backward, his face scarlet with fury. He took a step toward her, then stopped. He seemed puzzled as he swayed, then staggered to the side. As he started to crumple to the floor, Zoe dropped her coffee and grabbed him. She managed to shield his head from the table, but she couldn't stop him from hitting the floor.

"Wallace?" She unbuttoned his wool coat and put her hand on his chest, felt his heart beating way too fast. He tried to speak, but no sound came out of his mouth. His eyes were moving, but he didn't seem to see her. The coffee she'd dropped stained his coat and slacks, and the smell of it was sharp and bitter.

Looking up at the shocked faces surrounding her, she said, "Someone call 9-1-1."

* * *

THE LIGHT from the ambulance pulsed steadily outside the window of the coffee shop, a red heartbeat of anxiety. She closed her eyes to shut out the flashing. But it wouldn't go away. It bounced off the walls and into her brain, a steady, continual reminder of the last time she'd called for an ambulance.

She had to be dreaming. This couldn't be happening again.

Another Tate removed on a gurney.

Another police car stationed behind the ambulance.

What had happened to Wallace? She headed outside, intending to ask the paramedics. Why had he collapsed so suddenly? Was it a heart attack?

A blast of fresh spring air met her as she opened the door, and she stopped abruptly. Wallace Tate was on the gurney, parked at the back of the ambulance. Two paramedics labored over him. When they moved, she realized they'd been strapping him in.

She felt unexpected pity for the man who lay helpless in front of her. Wallace Tate, her nemesis for the past six years, reduced to a pathetic old man. Wallace would hate that. Her compassion would be unbearable to him. With one last look at the ambulance, she turned back into the shop.

"You watching the show, Zoe? Getting a kick out of it?"

Ray Dobbs, the chief of police, crowded behind her in the doorway. His blue eyes were cold and his gray buzz cut looked like a stiff brush. His whole body bristled with indignation.

"I was feeling sorry for Wallace," she said, holding his gaze. "Don't you think that's ironic?"

"I'm not finding much to laugh about."

"That's your problem, Chief. You don't have a sense of humor."

Dobbs flushed. "Watch your mouth, Zoe. You're already in enough trouble."

Zoe tried to hold on to her temper. "What do you mean? I have no idea what happened to Wallace."

"He just fell over." Dobbs's eyes glittered. "For no reason."

"Exactly." Despite her fear, Zoe steeled her face into an expression of polite interest. It was a talent she'd perfected during her marriage. "We were talking and he collapsed."

"Talking?" Dobbs edged closer, his expression hard with suspicion. "Is that what you call it?" He nodded to the other customers, milling around in small groups and murmuring to one another. "Maybe we should ask them if you were just 'talking.'"

"Wallace was angry. That shouldn't come as a shock to you. He's been angry with me for six years. He got a little loud."

"What were you 'talking' about?" Dobbs sneered.

Zoe dug her nails into her palms. "It was personal. It's no one else's business."

"You don't think so?" Dobbs moved so close she felt his breath on her face. "You better lose the attitude, or I'll toss your ass in a cell while we sort out what really happened."

"Don't think you can intimidate me, Chief. It's not going to work. Better men than you have tried, starting with Wallace Tate." Instead of moving away, she held her ground. She kept her gaze steady and concentrated on breathing evenly. "You can't arrest me because a man fell sick in front of me."

"Wallace was angry and you had a fight." Dobbs's mouth thinned.

"I didn't say that."

"He got in your face. Did you shove him? Is that why he fell down?"

"Of course not! I didn't touch him." But she had, she remembered with a burst of fear. She'd pushed his hand away.

Dobbs scanned the café. "Lots of witnesses here. Let's see what they have to say." He pointed to a chair. "Sit down. And stay there."

"I'm not going to sit down. You can't keep me here."

The chief of police turned red. "You're a pain in the ass. You know that, Zoe?"

"I get that a lot," Zoe said. "Mostly when men are trying to bully me to get at a woman in the shelter." She took a deep breath. She knew better than to let Dobbs push her buttons.

"Chief, the paramedic has a question for you." Jamie Evans, the patrol officer who'd responded to the 9-1-1 call, stepped into the shop. "He's outside."

Dobbs hitched up his navy blue uniform pants, then turned and walked out the door. As soon as he was gone, Zoe dropped into one of the old-fashioned wooden chairs. This wasn't like six years ago, she told herself. No one was dead and she hadn't done anything. There was nothing to worry about.

Except that Wallace Tate was involved. That changed everything.

She pulled her cell phone out of her jacket, watching Dobbs return and begin questioning the other customers. When her attorney answered, she said, "Helen, I have a problem. Wallace Tate collapsed while he was talking to me, and Dobbs is making noises about arresting me."

"What?" Her attorney's voice rose. "You got into a fight with Tate?"

"No!" Zoe reached down and picked up the coffee cup she'd dropped earlier. No one had mopped up the coffee. "He came into Joe's yelling at me, shook his finger in my face, then fell down. That's it."

"Don't say a word and don't lose your temper," Helen said sharply.

"Too late." Zoe watched the paramedics loading Wallace into the ambulance.

"Zoe, haven't you learned—" Helen bit off the words. "Sorry. Don't say anything else. If all you were doing was talking, Dobbs can't arrest you."

"That wouldn't stop him. Wallace is on his way to the hospital and Dobbs is scared. Who knows what he'll do?" Zoe swallowed. "I need you here, Helen."

"I'm thirty minutes away in Green Bay taking a deposition." Zoe heard her attorney shuffling papers. "It'll take me a couple of hours to finish up, but I'll get there as fast as I can."

"Hurry, Helen." As she spoke, Dobbs swung away from a table and headed toward her, his face triumphant. "I'm getting a bad feeling here."

"I'll call the office and see if anyone else is available. Hang on, Zoe. I won't let them lock you up."

"Okay," Zoe said, shuddering as she imagined the walls of a jail cell pressing in on her.

"Stay calm, Zoe."

"I'll try."

"Do better than try. Don't give Dobbs any more ammunition." Helen's voice was grim as she hung up.

Zoe closed the phone, took a deep breath and sat up straight as Dobbs reached her.

His eyes gleamed maliciously. "You said you didn't touch Wallace," he said. "You want to rethink that statement?"

"I didn't push him."

"That's not the story I'm hearing." He jerked his head toward two women who'd gone to high school with Zoe. They wouldn't meet her eyes. "Mary Ellen and Tina said you pushed him."

"They're wrong," Zoe said. She tried to control her growing panic.

"Witnesses say otherwise." He reached behind him and brought out handcuffs, which flashed in the light. "Zoe McInnes, you're under arrest…"

The scene with Wallace flashed in front of her again, and she swallowed. "He was shaking his finger in my face and I pushed it away. That's all."

"That's battery. And you're under arrest. Turn around." He dangled the handcuffs in front of her.

"Then you're going to have to arrest Wallace, too."

"Don't tell me how to do my job, McInnes."

"Someone has to. No judge will let you get away with this."

"Doesn't matter." Dobbs leaned closer and lowered his voice. "Maybe I can't hold you for more than a few hours, but that's enough to get your name in the paper. 'Zoe McInnes, head of Safe Harbor Women's Shelter, arrested for battery.' How's that sound? I think Wallace will like it."

Zoe stared at the police chief. "I know you're Wallace's main butt-kisser because you want him to give you a job at the college, but isn't this going a little too far, even for you, Chief? That shelter does a lot of good. It's where your police officers bring domestic-violence victims."

"You should have thought of that before you hit Wallace."

Why did Helen have to be in Green Bay today of all days? Zoe thought frantically as Dobbs grabbed her by the shoulder. He spun her around harder than necessary, and she stumbled. As she caught herself against the wall, Dobbs yanked her other hand behind her back.

"Chief? What's going on?" Jamie Evans, his dark blond hair ruffled by the wind, stepped between them.

Dobbs shoved him out of the way. "What the hell do you think?" He slammed a handcuff on one of her wrists and pulled it tight. The cold metal sent a chill through her. "I'm arresting her for battery. She shoved Wallace Tate and that's why he fell."

"That's not true," Zoe said hotly. "I did not push him."

Jamie put his hand on Dobbs's arm. "I know Wallace is a friend of yours," he said. "Why don't you calm down?"

"She's mouthing off to me," Dobbs said.

"I'm sure she is, but you can't put her in handcuffs just because she's giving you a hard time," Evans said. He frowned at Zoe. "And, you, keep your mouth shut."

She and Jamie had been friends forever. But she wasn't going to meekly submit, even for him. "Tell your boss to back off."

Jamie shifted so his body was between her and Dobbs. "There were no marks on Wallace, Chief. No sign she did anything to him. Maybe we should talk to the ER doc before this gets out of hand."

"*You* telling me how to do my job now, Evans?" Dobbs said. His low voice carried an unmistakable threat.

"I'm trying to save you from yourself."

"I don't need anybody saving me. She's going to cool her ass in a cell for a while."

"Chief, her lawyer is Helen Cherney. You know what kind of hell she can raise. Are you sure you want to do this?"

"Damn right, I'm sure." The chief glared at his subordinate. "Cherney may have you buffaloed, but she doesn't scare me."

"She should," Evans muttered as he turned away. Zoe glanced at Jamie. He and Helen had been dancing around each other for months. Apparently they hadn't gotten any further than exchanging barbs.

Dobbs yanked her other hand behind her back and secured it in the remaining cuff. Then he turned her around and marched her out the door. She glared at the other coffee shop patrons, who'd all been watching with avid interest. She knew almost everyone. Most of them suddenly became busy with their coffee or newspaper.

AN HOUR LATER, she paced circles in a holding cell in the Spruce Lake police station, her breath whistling in and out of her constricted throat. Her skin felt two sizes too small, and she wrapped her arms around herself to stop the shaking. If she'd known she was going to end up in jail, she thought wildly, she'd have worn something warmer than the silk blouse and lightweight pants.

The walls closed in more with each circuit, and she glanced at the clock on the wall again. The minute hand had barely moved.

Where was Helen? Or another attorney from her office? It had been more than two hours. She reached for her phone, then remembered they'd taken it away from her. Along with her watch, her messenger bag, her necklace and her earrings.

She stopped pacing to slap the metal bars in frustration, then sat on the thin mattress of the bed and pulled her knees up to her chin. She closed her eyes to block out the bright lights and willed herself somewhere far away from Spruce Lake.

At the sound of a door opening, she raised her head. A tall, dark-haired man stepped into the corridor. He wore a suit and carried a briefcase. Zoe jumped off the cot.

"Thank goodness," she said, hurrying over to him. "Did you get this straightened out? Were you able to talk some sense into Ray Dobbs?" She gripped the bars. "I need to get out of this cage."

One of the young police officers she barely knew came into the corridor behind the man and opened the cell door. The man stepped inside, the police officer locked the door behind him and disappeared again.

The attorney's gaze moved slowly over her, from head to toe. "You're Zoe McInnes?" His deep voice sounded almost accusing.

"Of course I am." She swept her hand around the empty cell. "There's no one else back here, is there?"

"You want to tell me what happened with Wallace?"

"I'll tell you whatever you want. Just get me out of here."

"Why would I do that?"

Zoe stared at him. "Because that's your job! Helen sent you over, didn't she?"

"Helen who?"

Zoe's stomach lurched. "You're not an attorney?"

"I am, but I don't know anyone named Helen."

Zoe took a deep breath, then looked at the man again. He seemed vaguely familiar, but she couldn't place him. "Who are you?"

He studied her for a moment longer. Finally he said, "I'm Gideon Tate. Wallace's other son." His hand tightened on his briefcase. "The one you didn't kill."

CHAPTER TWO

THE WOMAN STANDING in front of him paled, making her black hair and bright blue eyes even more vivid. Her hand tightened on the bar, then dropped away as she stared at him. If he hadn't known who she was, he would have said she looked hurt.

"You're Derrick's brother?"

"In the flesh."

"What are you doing here, Mr. Tate?" she asked.

He watched as she struggled to pull herself together. In a few seconds, the desperate, pleading woman had disappeared, replaced by a cool, collected one. It was hard to believe she was the same person who'd begged him to get her out of the cell.

"I came to see the woman who caused my father's stroke."

"Wallace had a stroke?"

"That's what the doctors said."

He saw relief flicker across her face. "I'm sorry to hear that."

She was a damn good actress. But he already knew that—he'd watched her performance at the trial six years ago. "I want to know why he had a stroke."

"I have no idea. I heard he has high blood pressure. Maybe he forgot to take his medication." She quirked one eyebrow, and his anger swelled. She was a cold piece of work.

"What happened while he was talking to you?" Gideon leaned forward, surprised when she didn't flinch or back away. He'd been told he was intimidating. "Did you say something to make him angry?"

To his surprise, she smiled. "You must not know your father very well if you need to ask that. My very existence infuriates him."

Staring at Zoe McInnes, he understood that feeling very well. "What specific thing infuriated him this time?"

Her smile disappeared. "I'm sorry, but that's none of your business."

"Yes, it is. My father had a stroke because of it."

She shrugged. "You can ask Wallace. But I'm sure he won't tell you, either."

"I have no intention of asking my father anything."

"Then I guess you're never going to know."

"You're pretty damn cocky for someone sitting in a jail cell."

"If Wallace had a stroke, I won't be here much longer. The last I heard, there's no law against being in the same room when someone becomes ill."

He was antagonizing her. Time to be smart and use the charm everyone said he possessed. "Ms. McInnes, I didn't come here to fight with you. I just want to ask you a few questions."

She studied him for a moment, then shrugged. "Why not? I can't exactly walk away from you, can I?" She rubbed at her lower arm, and when her hand dropped away, he saw angry red lines around both her wrists.

He nodded at the marks. "How did that happen?"

She glanced at her wrists. "Handcuffs."

"Really? Let me see." He set his briefcase on the floor and reached for her arm, and she flinched away from him. Letting his hand drop to his side, he said, "Your attorney should talk to the police chief about that."

Her mouth curved. "Don't worry, she will."

He wondered about a woman who could plead to be let out of a cell, but ignore bruises caused by handcuffs. Again, she surprised him by returning his stare. He was Derrick's brother, after all, and she'd murdered Derrick. But she watched Gideon defiantly, as if daring him to challenge her.

"Ray Dobbs told me that you and my father had a fight in the coffee shop."

She leaned against the bars of the cell but didn't back down. "Wallace doesn't fight with people. He tells them what to do and expects them to obey."

"What did my father want you to do?"

"Knuckle under to him. And that's not going to happen." She held his gaze steadily. "Wallace doesn't like it when people tell him no. Maybe that's why he had a stroke."

He knew that aspect of his father's personality all too well. "He's not an easy man."

"That's the understatement of the year." She pushed away from the bars. "What have the doctors said?"

"Not a lot. They're still doing tests. Apparently he's having trouble speaking and moving."

"That doesn't sound good. Poor Wallace."

How the hell did she manage to sound sincere? Gideon wished he was anywhere but in this jail cell with this woman. Her false sympathy got under his skin. "They found a blood clot on the CT scan and they're treating it. He's lucky they got him to the hospital right away. But the lack of movement and speech is a concern. It'll take a couple of days to figure out how bad the damage is."

"I'm sorry. But I still can't tell you what we were talking about."

"Why the hell not?"

"Because it involves another person." She turned and began pacing again, keeping a careful distance between them. "I hope your father recovers quickly, Mr. Tate. I know he'll get excellent care at Spruce Lake Hospital."

He didn't move. "Why are you still here?"

She yanked at one of the bars. "Because Ray Dobbs didn't trust me with a key."

"I mean in this town."

She smoothed her hand down her leg as she watched him. Finally, she said, "As I'm sure you know, I had to serve my probation in Spruce Lake. By the time it was finished, I'd made a life for myself. One I wasn't willing to give up."

"So you stay here and remind everyone of what you did."

"No. I'm reminding everyone of what your brother did."

"And how are you doing that?"

She smiled. "I started a shelter for victims of domestic violence, using the money I got when I sold our house."

"Talk about twisting the knife. Could you make my father hate you any more?"

Her smile faded. "He hates me because he can't bully me."

"He hates you for what you did to his son. I never believed that Derrick beat you. That he abused you. He was my brother. I knew him."

"Is that right?" She straightened, and even though she was smaller than he was, it felt like she was looking down her nose at him. "You never saw him in the two years we were married. You didn't even come to our wedding."

"I couldn't make it."

She shook her head. "He was your brother. You could have been there for him."

She had the nerve to judge him? "My relationship with Derrick was complicated."

"He was only your half brother." She gave him a brittle smile. "I guess that doesn't count as much."

"That had nothing to do with it." But it had. He hadn't needed his father or Derrick, because he'd had his mother and a great stepfather.

He'd carried the guilt of his neglect since the day he'd gotten the phone call about Derrick's death.

"Whatever you say." Her gaze was challenging, as if she wanted him to argue with her.

"I was busy," he said dismissively. Even to him, it sounded lame.

"So was Derrick," she retorted. "He was busy beating me."

As if perfectly cued, the door opened and a blond woman hurried toward the cell. She was dressed in a suit and carried a briefcase. "Sorry it took so long, Zoe." She stopped. "Who the hell are you?" she said to him.

"I'm Gideon Tate. Wallace's other son."

"The one I didn't kill," Zoe added.

So that had stung. Good, he thought.

"What are you doing in there with her?"

"I wanted to talk to her."

"And Dobbs just let you in?"

He shrugged. "I guess I asked nicely."

Her eyes narrowed. "Dobbs is an even bigger fool than I thought he was."

Zoe moved past him, trailing a citrusy scent that was grotesquely out of place in this cell where the air smelled of sour sweat and desperation. "Get me out of here, Helen."

"They're just finishing the paperwork." She reached through the bar and took Zoe's hand. "Hold on for another five minutes."

The two women ignored him as they spoke in low voices, and he took the opportunity to study Zoe McInnes. She looked a lot different than she had at her trial. Then, her long, wavy black hair had been pulled back into a neat twist every day. Her eyes had been carefully blank, impossible to read. And she'd been painfully thin, almost sticklike in her royal blue suit. It had hung off her as if she was a child playing dress-up with her mother's clothes.

Today her short, dark hair curled around her face, a dramatic frame for her eyes. Instead of skinny, she looked fit and well-toned. And he hadn't had any trouble reading her eyes—they held amusement, cool composure and an "I don't give a damn" attitude that stirred his anger.

The door to the corridor opened again, and a uniformed officer headed toward them. "Move that toy you drive, Helen," he said. "It's obstructing our squad cars."

Helen waited for him to unlock the cell, then she pulled Zoe out. "That's too damn bad, Jamie." She smiled at the officer. "But we'll be out of your way soon. It's not going to take long for your boss to make a fool out of himself."

She towed Zoe into the bullpen of the police station, and Gideon trailed behind. They were halfway across the room when Ray Dobbs stepped out of his office and into their path.

"Look who's here," Dobbs said with a sneer. "Spruce Lake's own hotshot attorney."

"Hello to you, too, Chief." Helen planted herself in front of Zoe, who immediately stepped up next to her. Apparently Zoe McInnes didn't let anyone fight her battles. "You really screwed up this time."

"Wow. There's a surprise," Zoe said.

Helen rounded on Zoe. "I told you to keep your mouth shut," she said. "You're supposed to take my advice—that's why you pay me the big bucks. And if you can't keep quiet, at least remember the rule—if we're playing good cop, bad cop, I get to be the bad cop."

"Don't you ever get tired of being a hard-ass, Helen?" Jamie asked, leaning against the wall.

She held the officer's gaze for a long moment, then smiled. "Nah. It's too much fun." Turning to Dobbs, she asked, "Have you talked to anyone at the emergency room about Wallace?"

"No, I haven't. I've been too busy at the crime scene."

"You're losing your touch, Ray," Helen said, shaking her head. "It's no fun when you make my job so easy." She glanced at Zoe, nodded slightly. "I talked to Luke Trenton, the neurologist at the hospital. He says Wallace had a stroke." She looked at Gideon. "That right, Tate?"

"That's what I was told," Gideon answered.

"There you go." Helen turned back to the police chief. "We're out of here, Dobbs."

Dobbs's expression hardened. "A stroke?"

"Yes."

Dobbs stepped too close to Zoe. "Far as I'm concerned, you caused that stroke. You better hope he recovers." The chief stormed out of the room.

Helen smiled, linked her arm through Zoe's and led her toward the lobby.

"Wait a minute," Gideon said. "I'm not finished talking to Ms. McInnes."

The two women stopped. "Do you want to talk to him?" the attorney asked Zoe.

"No."

"You're done, Tate."

Anger churned inside him, but he kept his face impassive. "I'll catch up with you later, Ms. McInnes."

"I have nothing more to say to you, Mr. Tate," Zoe answered. Her eyes were steady on his, but he couldn't read her gaze.

He strode past them and out the main entrance. Zoe's attorney was wrong. They were far from done.

ZOE LET OUT a shaky breath as the door clicked shut behind Gideon. As soon as he was gone, Helen asked, "What happened, Zoe?"

Instead of answering, Zoe nodded in Jamie Evans's direction. He'd followed them into the lobby. "I'm gone," he said, heading for the door. He winked at Helen as he passed them. "So long, tough girl."

"That man gets on my nerves," Helen muttered.

"Yeah, I've noticed," Zoe answered. She headed toward the exit. "I need to get out of here, Helen."

The lawyer held her back. "Take it easy," she said. "We stroll out slowly. Like we have all day. Dobbs is going to be watching from his office. Don't let him see you sweating."

Zoe's chest tightened. "I don't have all day."

Helen linked her arm through Zoe's, making her walk at a normal pace. "Yeah, Zoe, you do."

Somehow she managed to leave the police station like a normal person, someone who didn't freak out and lose control when confined in a small space. She took a deep breath of the fresh, chilly spring air as they headed toward Helen's sports car, sitting in front of the station in a No Parking zone.

As Helen zoomed away from the station, she said, "All right, Zoe. Tell me exactly what happened."

Zoe recounted the argument she'd had with Wallace Tate. "He just fell to the floor," she finished.

"Did you touch him?"

Zoe watched the downtown Spruce Lake shops flash past the window. "He was sticking his finger in my face." *Just like his son Derrick used to do.*

"Did you touch him?" Helen's voice was flat.

"I pushed his finger away," Zoe said. "That's all."

"For God's sake, Zoe! You couldn't control yourself?"

"I didn't knock him down, Helen." Now that she was out of the cell and the police station, energy leaked out of her like air out of a balloon. "He had a stroke. That's not my fault."

"Of course it isn't. But Dobbs isn't going to see it that way."

"I don't give a damn about Dobbs. I didn't do anything wrong." She glared at her attorney. "I was in the coffee shop, minding my own business. He came after me, threatening me. He was poking his finger in my face. All I did was push it away."

Helen's expression softened. "Take it easy, Zoe. I'm not saying you did anything wrong. I'm just trying to think like Dobbs."

"That's impossible. Dobbs doesn't think. He lets Wallace do that for him."

Helen tucked a strand of her blond hair behind her ear and laughed. "This town would be dull as ditch water without you, Zo."

Zoe grimaced. "I'd rather be dull," she said. "I'd love it if no one in this town knew my name."

Helen's smile faded as she pulled up behind Zoe's car, still in the parking lot of Joe's Coffee House. "Whatever happens with Dobbs and Wallace, you don't have to face it alone this time. At least Bree and Fiona are here."

"Right." Zoe jumped out of the car. Her sisters might be in town, but that didn't mean all was sweetness and light in the McInnes family. There was too much painful history between them, too much anger, too many tears. She loved her sisters, but the three of them together inevitably butted heads. It had been that way since they were children, always two against one. The two changed, usually daily, but the tension was always there.

Encouraged by their father.

The novelty of being triplets in a small town, of drawing stares and murmured words wherever they went, hadn't helped. Neither had their father's almost pathological need for attention. "They're not here because of me. They're here to clean out our father's house so we can sell it."

Helen slammed the car door and hurried after her. "It doesn't matter why they're here. You shut them out six years ago when Derrick died," she said, clutching Zoe's hand. "They're still hurt about that. Now's your chance to make it up to them." She tightened her grip. "You'd want to support them if they were in trouble."

"But I'm not in trouble. Wallace had a stroke. I had

nothing to do with it. End of story." She pulled her hand away from Helen.

The attorney stepped in front of Zoe before she could get into her car. "Do you really think this is the end of the story, Zo? You know how bad Dobbs wants that job at the college, and Wallace is the man who can hire him. He'd lock you up again in a heartbeat if he thought it would curry favor with Wallace Tate."

Zoe's hand shook as she unlocked the car door, and Helen pressed. "Now Derrick's brother is in town. What does he want from you, Zoe? Have you thought about that? The gossips are going to have a field day with him confronting you in the jail."

"I don't need Bree and Fiona to face down the gossips for me."

"Maybe they want to," Helen answered. Zoe slid into her car and Helen grabbed the door to keep her from closing it. "Maybe they need to. Go talk to your sisters, Zoe. Have a glass of wine, make dinner together. I'll see what I can find out about Wallace. And his son Gideon."

As Helen walked away, Zoe pulled out her cell phone. She had one text message waiting. Opening the phone, she saw it was from her sister Bree. "RU alright?" it said. "What's wrong?"

CHAPTER THREE

"ANYONE HERE?" Zoe called as she stepped into the old Victorian house. It smelled of fresh air and window cleaner, and she paused for a moment to drink in the aromas. Her father's house had been shut up and stale even before he'd died six months ago. Since her sisters had been back, it felt as if someone actually lived in it.

"We're in the kitchen," Bree called.

Zoe made her way past a bag of tree-bark bedding for Charlie's reptiles and a stack of empty boxes in the hall to the back of the house. Fiona, her face the mirror image of Zoe's, was talking on her cell phone, and Bree was standing at the sink, peeling a cucumber. The sunlight streaming in through the window made Bree's red hair glitter like gold. She smiled at Zoe over her shoulder. "Are you okay?" she asked. "I was worried."

"I saw your text message," Zoe answered. "That was weird."

Bree shrugged. "We used to know when something had happened to one of us. Remember?"

"I do," Fiona said. She closed her cell phone. "When Bree said she was worried about you, I thought of Derrick. Then I remembered I don't have to worry about him anymore."

Zoe dropped into a kitchen chair. "You guys are freaking me out."

"Why?" Bree asked, turning toward her.

Zoe took a deep breath, but before she could tell her sisters about Wallace and Gideon, Charlie skidded through the back door.

"Mom! Did you hear what happened?"

"Say hi to your aunts," Bree said automatically.

"Hi, Aunt Fee," he said as Fiona hugged him. His eyes widened. "Aunt Zo! How did you get out of jail?"

"Jail?" Fiona dropped her phone onto the table. *"Jail?"*

Bree slammed the refrigerator door. "What are you talking about, Charlie?"

"Ray Dobbs arrested me today," Zoe said.

Charlie pumped his fist. "Yes! Logan bet me it was a lie. Now he owes me five bucks."

"For God's sake, Charlie," Bree said.

Zoe choked back a laugh. "I'm glad I made you some money today, kid." She explained to her sisters what had happened. "That's why your text message was so eerie, Bree." She glanced at Fiona. "And you thinking about Derrick. His brother Gideon showed up at the jail." She forced a smile. "I guess the old woo-woo connection is still there."

"It was just a little rusty," Bree said quietly.

"Derrick's brother was there? And Dobbs let him see you?" Fiona frowned.

"Yes. We had an interesting conversation. After he said I'd murdered his brother, he wanted to know what I'd done to his father."

"The bastard," Bree said hotly. "I should kick Ray Dobbs's ass for letting him in to see you."

Fiona pushed away from the table. "Nothing's changed in this town at all. Now do you understand why I don't want to be here?"

"It isn't the whole town," Zoe said, irritation creeping into her voice. "Ray Dobbs is a bully and he's targeting me because he wants Wallace to give him a cushy job at the college. That doesn't mean everyone else in Spruce Lake is a jerk."

"It doesn't bother you that the chief of police is a bully who arrests people so he can get a better job?" Fiona retorted.

"Of course it does. But I'm not going to blame the whole town."

"How can you stand to live here, Zoe?" Fiona demanded. "They kept you in jail for nine months and tried to send you to prison for killing a man who was beating you to death."

"That nine months gave birth to the shelter. I'm doing a lot of good in Spruce Lake," Zoe replied quietly, pouring herself a glass of orange juice. "I'm helping a lot of women." Even if sometimes she wanted to disappear into the anonymity of a larger city. Just like Fiona had done. "I have friends here."

"Clearly, not where they count," Fiona said.

"I'm going to go talk to Ray Dobbs," Bree declared, scooping up the cucumber peels and putting them in the compost pail. "I'll make him leave you alone."

Zoe turned to her. "Don't, Bree. I know you mean well, but that would just make it worse, trust me. Ray would like nothing better than to have another McInnes woman in his sights."

"You can't let him get away with this," Bree said.

"It's okay, Helen Cherney is taking care of things."

Zoe forced a smile. "Do you guys know Helen? She was several years ahead of us in school."

They talked about other classmates for a while and finally Zoe was able to breathe normally again. She didn't want to entangle her sisters in her problems.

"Hey, Bree, I think I may have a lead on a substitute-teaching job for you," Zoe said when the subject of old friends petered out.

"Yeah?" Bree's eyes lit up. "Somewhere close?"

"As close as you can get. Spruce Lake High. One of the English teachers is in my shelter and I know the school is having a hard time finding a qualified sub. Why don't you go talk to the principal tomorrow?"

Bree's smile disappeared. "Spruce Lake is a little too close." She glanced at Charlie, who had peeled an orange and was eating it over the sink. "Charlie, go wash your hands and get started on your homework."

When her son was out of earshot, Bree continued. "Someone here in Spruce Lake will have heard about my 'moral turpitude.'" Bree made quotation marks with her fingers. "I don't want to be humiliated again."

Fiona paused as she punched a number into her cell phone. "No one in Spruce Lake knows what you did while you were in college," she said.

"I didn't think anyone in Milwaukee knew, either," Bree retorted. "But the school board found out somehow. They will here, too. You know how small towns are." She sighed. "As much as I'd love to get a job at Spruce Lake High, I don't think so."

Bree scooped her long hair away from her face, twining a curl around her finger as she searched for a clip to hold it in place. Even as a child, Bree had played with her hair when she was nervous. "That was a long time ago, Bree," Zoe said. "You were so young. You were trying to take care of your child and go to school at the same time. People will understand."

"Yeah, just like they understood when you shot Derrick, right, Zoe?"

"That was different."

"Yeah," Bree said, smoothing her baggy T-shirt over her hips. "You don't think people here are going to care if an ex-stripper is teaching their children? Get real, Zoe."

"At least think about it," Zoe begged. Her sister was out of work, and Spruce Lake High would be so convenient. "Go and talk to the principal. That doesn't commit you to taking the job."

"You haven't changed, have you, Zo?" Bree said, leaning against the counter. "You're still bossing us around."

"I'm trying to help you!" Zoe retorted.

"Maybe I don't need your help," Bree flashed back.

"You need a job. I'm giving you a heads-up on one."

"Hey, Bree, you're not going to be here forever," Fiona pointed out from her seat at the kitchen table. "So if they find out, you can just leave again."

"Fiona, running away isn't always the answer. Sometimes you have to face people down." Zoe looked at her sister, so much like herself, yet she barely recognized her.

"Maybe we're not as strong as you, Zoe," Fiona said quietly. "Sometimes running away is the only choice." She snapped her phone closed. "I have to fly back to New York. Something's come up."

"We've barely started on the house," Zoe said.

"I'm not leaving for a few days. And I'll be back. There's a jewelry show at a store here in Spruce Lake next week that I have to go to." She made a production of sliding her phone into the pocket of her jeans.

"What's more important than this?" Bree asked.

"I have to meet with some department-store buyers. My manager arranged it. It's a big deal." She didn't look at either of her sisters. "I promise I'll come back."

"Fiona, I didn't think you wanted to sell your jewelry in department stores," Zoe said.

"You *are* still bossy, aren't you?" Fiona retorted.

"I confront problems, Fee. I don't run away from them." She and Fiona might look identical, but they couldn't be more different.

"It's just like the good old days, isn't it?" Bree said, pushing away from the counter. "Putting us in the same room is like putting three cats in a bag."

"We're not that bad," Zoe said lightly. It was just bickering. Heaven knew they'd been bickering for twenty years. But she'd hoped it would be different. She'd hoped they'd all grown up. Now Fiona was running away again. Just like she had before. "Okay, Fee," she said quietly. "Go back to New York. Take care of your business. But please come home when you're done."

Fiona's eyes flickered when Zoe said "home." But she nodded. "I will."

She hurried out of the room, and Zoe looked at Bree. She knew her sister was thinking the same thing— would Fiona come back?

She wasn't sure.

GIDEON STOOD next to the hospital bed and stared down at the motionless man. His father's eyes tracked him and his mouth moved, but he didn't speak. Wallace's hair was white and his putty-gray skin sagged at the jowls and neck. He'd gotten old in the six years since Derrick's death.

"Hi, Dad," Gideon said in a low voice. "They called me and said you'd had a stroke, so I drove up yesterday." His hands tightened on the bed rail. "I'll stick around for a while and make sure they take good care of you."

His father opened his mouth but only garbled sounds came out. Was the old man grateful he was here? Or was he trying to tell Gideon to leave?

It didn't matter. He wasn't going anywhere. His father's rejection so many years ago had hurt, but Gideon was an adult now. He should have been man enough to make the first move long ago.

This was his chance to put things right. He hadn't intended to return to Spruce Lake, ever, but when he'd gotten the call, he'd headed north. There was no one else to speak for his father. No one else to make sure Zoe McInnes paid for what she'd done.

It wasn't enough that she'd killed his brother. Now she'd caused his father to have a stroke. This time, he wasn't going to leave Spruce Lake until she'd been punished.

"Ray Dobbs arrested Zoe McInnes," he told the still figure on the bed. There was a flash in his father's eyes that might have been pleasure. "If she's responsible for this, I'll make sure she pays for it."

Wallace tried to speak. Watching helplessly, Gideon reached for his hand. He covered it with his own, and his father's fingers twitched. Wallace's skin felt dry and fragile. An old man's hand.

"Hi, there." A voice came from behind him, and Gideon drew his hand away from his father's. A man about Gideon's age in surgical scrubs moved to the end of the bed, holding a chart and watching Wallace intently. "I'm Dr. Trenton. You must be Wallace's son—I heard you were here. How's he doing this morning? Has he spoken to you?"

"No," Gideon answered. "His mouth moves and he makes some noises, but that's all."

The doctor scribbled something on the chart. "How about movement?"

"I felt his fingers move a little."

"His left hand?"

"Yes," Gideon replied.

"It's his left side that's affected." The doctor made more notes on the chart. Then turned to Gideon. "Would you mind waiting in the hall while I examine him?"

"Not at all."

It was a long time before the doctor came out. "The drug we gave him helped, but I'd like to inject some anti-clotting drugs directly into the obstruction," he said. "I was hoping to see more improvement today. I'll schedule the procedure for this afternoon."

"Is he going to be okay?"

Trenton hesitated. "I hope so," he finally said. "He's better than he was when he first came in. If we can dissolve more of the clot, he'll improve more quickly. He has some tough rehab in front of him, but I think he'll regain a fair amount of function. The CT scan didn't show anything that would prevent a pretty good recovery." He glanced at the chart, then slid it into the holder at the end of the bed. "Right now, I'm focused on trying to obliterate the clot."

Trenton turned to go, but Gideon said, "I need to ask you a question, Doctor. My father was having an argument with someone when he collapsed. Could that have caused this stroke?"

"I heard about that," Trenton said. "He was yelling at Zoe McInnes in the coffee shop. At least twenty different people have told me the story." He shook his head. "Hard to believe that many people could squeeze into Joe's."

"I guess small towns never change," Gideon said with a stiff smile. "Gossip moves at the speed of light."

"No kidding," Trenton said. He rocked back on his heels. "Could an argument have caused his stroke? It probably didn't help. But Wallace's high blood pressure is the real culprit."

"So the police chief won't be able to charge Zoe with anything?"

The doctor shrugged. "He could argue that the fight was a contributing factor. Whether it would stick or not is another matter." Trenton headed for the door. "I'm guessing Dobbs doesn't care, though. He's still mad that Zoe got away with killing—" The doctor stopped abruptly and slid his eyes away from Gideon. "Her husband," he finally said.

"My brother." Gideon fought back his anger.

Trenton looked him in the eye. "She said he'd been beating her and she was afraid for her life. Some people believed her."

The doctor moved down the hall and disappeared into another room as Gideon watched. Was the doctor one of the believers?

A picture of Zoe with her chin in the air and her straight back floated into his mind. She wasn't at all what he'd expected. The beaten-down ghost of a woman who'd sat silently at her trial had vanished. The woman he'd faced in that jail yesterday had been confident, assured and composed—once she'd realized who he was.

She'd seemed vulnerable and scared when he first walked into the cell. How had she managed to collect herself so quickly?

It hinted at depths to Zoe McInnes he didn't want to think about. She was the woman who'd killed his brother and now caused his father to have a stroke. That was all he needed to know about her.

All he needed to challenge her again. He'd find a way through her defenses. What had been so important to Wallace that he'd confronted the woman in public? He was determined to find out.

It was the least he could do for his father after ignoring him for so many years.

CHAPTER FOUR

GIDEON STRODE up the walk to his father's front door, brushing past the prickly overgrown juniper. It was a damn ugly plant, and he'd hated it since the time he'd fallen into it as a kid.

Junipers always made him think of his father's house.

Gideon opened the door of the old Georgian and reluctantly stepped inside. It felt as if he was betraying his mother by staying here.

The mahogany table beneath the mirror in the tiny entryway was exactly where it had been the last time he'd visited, more than twenty years ago. The overstuffed chair and couch in the living room were the same, too, although the upholstery had faded from the original purple to maroon.

Shoving his hands into his pockets, he walked into the kitchen. He was a trespasser in this house. An intruder. It wasn't home. He didn't remember his life here—his mother had divorced Wallace when Gideon was only a year old.

The kitchen smelled faintly of decay. He traced the odor to the wastebasket and carried the contents out to the garbage can. Then he sorted the mail.

His father's reading glasses lay on the counter. The previous day's newspaper was stacked in a neat pile on one of the kitchen chairs. A coffee mug and a plate and knife sat in the drainer by the sink. Normal, homey bits of a life. His father hadn't known when he walked out of the house yesterday that he wouldn't be coming back anytime soon.

Gideon wandered upstairs and picked up the mystery he'd left on the nightstand in the guest bedroom. There were ghosts everywhere. His mother, asking why he'd come back here. His father, asking why he'd left Spruce Lake with his mother when he was twelve, rather than stay with him and his half brother. His own guilt, asking himself why he hadn't been back.

Dropping the book, Gideon hurried down the stairs and into the late-afternoon sunlight. He took a deep breath of the air.

Maybe he'd go to the coffee shop where his father had collapsed and see if anyone had witnessed Wallace's confrontation with Zoe McInnes.

Walking down the main street of Spruce Lake, he heard a man say, "Gideon? Is that you?"

He turned and saw his brother's longtime friend Dave Johnson. "Hey, Dave. Good to see you."

Dave shook his hand, holding on a little too long. A little too hard. "Did you get my message?"

"Message?" Gideon realized he hadn't checked his voice mail since he'd been back in Spruce Lake.

"I called you when I heard what happened to your dad. I figured you'd come home."

"Sorry, Dave. I haven't listened to my messages since I arrived. It's been crazy."

Dave brushed his hand over his receding hairline. His face looked pinched. "Sorry about your dad."

The words sounded like an afterthought, and Gideon looked at him more carefully. "Are you okay?"

The other man stilled for a moment, then slowly shook his head. "No. I'm not."

"What's going on?" Gideon asked. Dave had been Derrick's best friend. Gideon had run into Dave while attending the University of Wisconsin at Madison, and they'd gotten reacquainted. Gideon hadn't kept up with him after Derrick died, but he remembered Dave as easygoing and laid-back. He never worried about anything.

Dave said, "Look, I know you're busy with your dad, but I need to talk to you. Do you have time for a beer?"

"Sure," Gideon said. "I don't have any plans." He could check out the coffee shop anytime.

When they walked into The Lake House it was almost deserted. Gideon glanced at the old canoes on the wall, the stuffed walleyes and northerns, the antique fishing rods. "I remember this place."

Dave managed a weary smile. "It's a Spruce Lake institution." He ordered two Leinenkugels from Jerry, the bartender, then they slid into a corner booth.

"How's Barb doing?" Gideon asked. He'd met Barb once or twice and he remembered an attractive, pleasant woman who'd seemed happy with her husband.

Dave took a drink of his beer. "That's what I wanted to talk to you about."

"Barb?"

"Yeah." Dave took another long swallow, and his hand trembled a little when he set the bottle on the table. "She told the police I'd been beating her and had me arrested."

"What?" Gideon froze, his beer halfway to his mouth. "Were you?"

"Was I what?"

"Beating Barb."

"Of course not." Dave looked insulted that he'd asked, and Gideon felt a twinge of guilt. Dave was his brother's friend. He should trust him to tell the truth.

"Why would she say that?"

"I have no idea," Dave said.

"Did she move out? Or did you?"

"She did. She's at the Safe Harbor Women's Shelter. Zoe McInnes is the one who called the police."

"Zoe McInnes?" Gideon slammed his bottle down with a bang.

"Yeah," Dave said impatiently. "Zoe runs the shelter. Now I'm facing spousal battery charges."

"But you didn't hit her."

"Of course not." Dave took another pull from his beer. "I'd never hurt Barb."

"She had to have some kind of proof," Gideon said. "The cops couldn't just arrest you on her say-so."

"Barb had fallen off a ladder," Dave said bitterly. "She bruised her arm and her side and cracked a couple of ribs. She told the cops I'd done it."

"Her word against yours."

"Exactly."

Gideon sat back, studying the other man. In his job as an assistant district attorney in Milwaukee, Gideon prosecuted spousal battery all the time. At least Dave was original. The usual excuse was "She fell down the stairs." It was followed closely by "She walked into a door."

"What do you want me to do?" Gideon asked.

Dave leaned forward, his eyes desperate. "You know how the system works. I want to hire you to defend me."

"I'm a prosecutor, Dave. I don't do defense work."

"You're a lawyer, aren't you?"

"Yes, but I'm usually on the other side of the aisle. In Milwaukee, I'd be the one prosecuting you. You need to find someone in town who knows how to mount a defense."

Dave finished his beer. "You think I'm guilty, don't you? You think I beat Barb."

Gideon slid his own bottle of beer from hand to hand across the polished table. If it was anyone but Dave, he would assume the guy was guilty. But Dave had been Derrick's friend. The least Gideon could do was keep an open mind about him. "You're saying she lied to the police. Why would she do that?" he asked.

"I don't know," Dave said, anguished. "I didn't realize she hated me that much. We had our problems. What couple doesn't? But this came totally out of the blue."

"Nothing precipitated it? You didn't push her during a fight? Threaten her?"

"I swear to you, Gideon, I didn't touch Barb." Dave slumped in his chair and wiped his palm across his face. "You remember my mom, don't you? How she was? If I ever so much as looked at a girl the wrong way, she'd ground me for a week. I've never hit a woman. Never could."

Gideon knew perfectly well that clients lied to their attorneys all the time. But Dave looked ashamed. Gideon rarely saw shame in the eyes of the men he prosecuted for spousal abuse.

"Tell me more about what's going on," Gideon said. "Why did Barb go to Zoe?"

"Safe Harbor is the only shelter in Spruce Lake. And Zoe will walk through fire for the women in it. Everyone in town knows that."

"Zoe doesn't question the women who show up?"

Gideon asked. "She doesn't make sure they're telling the truth?"

Dave shrugged. "I have no idea what she does. All I know is, when I tried to talk to Barb, Zoe shut me down. Wouldn't even listen to my side of the story. She told me Barb didn't want to have anything to do with me, and that was that." He motioned to the bartender for another beer. "She said she'd see me in court."

Gideon sipped his beer as Dave drained another bottle. Maybe this was just the tool he needed to pry some answers from Zoe. It would be the perfect excuse to seek her out. He wouldn't put it past her to be using the women's shelter to further her own agenda. If she was, he would take great pleasure in exposing her to the world.

He wanted to make her pay for what she'd done to his brother, and now his father, and Dave was handing him the opportunity.

"Okay, Dave. I'll take your case."

"THANKS FOR BRINGING Marilu and her daughter to me," Zoe said to Jamie Evans. She nodded at the corkboard in her office that held photos of smiling women and children. All of them had stayed at her shelter. "Now she has a chance to get her life together and be happy."

Jamie's lips thinned. "I'm just glad she finally got away from that bastard Jesse Halvorsen," he said. "It's about time. And you be careful, too. Halvorsen has an ugly temper, and he doesn't like being crossed." He studied the pictures that decorated her walls—crayon drawings from children who'd found safety here. "As many times as I see it, I still can't understand how anyone can hit his own wife and kid."

"That's why you're a good cop, Jamie." Zoe sifted

through the papers and books on her desk until she found one of Helen's cards. "Marilu needs an attorney, but she doesn't have any money." Zoe held out the card to Jamie. "Helen Cherney knows Jesse and Marilu. I bet she'd take the case pro bono. Why don't you go talk to her?"

Jamie drummed his fingers on the desk and avoided her eyes. "Helen would probably refuse to have anything to do with Marilu if I went to see her."

Zoe smiled. "You might be surprised." She leaned forward and shoved the card into Jamie's hand. His fingers closed around it.

"I know where her office is," he muttered.

"Then go talk to her. She doesn't bite, you know."

"Oh, yeah?" Jamie eased out of the chair. "Then why do I have teeth marks on my ass from the last time I tangled with her?"

The phone rang as Zoe locked the door of the shelter behind Jamie. "Safe Harbor Shelter."

"May I speak to Zoe McInnes?" a male voice said.

Zoe tightened her grip on the phone. She knew that voice. "This is Zoe."

"Ms. McInnes, it's Gideon Tate. I need to talk to you."

"Is this about Wallace?" *Please, God, he's not worse.* "Is he improving?"

"My father's condition hasn't changed. This has nothing to do with him."

Zoe bit back a sigh of relief. One less thing to worry about right now. "What is it, then?"

"It's regarding your shelter."

"Safe Harbor? What about it?" she asked warily. If a Tate was involved, it wouldn't be good.

"I'd rather not discuss it over the phone. May I come to your office?"

"Sorry, but no," Zoe said. "Men I don't know personally aren't allowed in the shelter."

"Then I'll meet you somewhere."

Impatience flared in his voice, and Zoe leaned back in her chair, her own temper stirring. "I'm sorry, Mr. Tate, but my schedule is very full. I might be able to find time for you—" she leafed through her appointment book "—in two days."

"What time?"

Zoe looked at Friday's blank page. "I could probably fit you in around three," she said. "I'll meet you at Joe's Coffee House." The place where Wallace had confronted her. Talking to Gideon there would banish some of the ghosts. Give her more control.

There was a heavy pause, then Gideon said, "I'll look forward to seeing you soon." He hung up.

Pleased, Zoe replaced the phone. The next time she met with a Tate, it would be on her terms.

THE REMNANTS of an early-spring thunderstorm rumbled in the distance as Zoe pulled into her driveway a couple of hours later. A light rain continued to fall as she made her way carefully across the wet pavers to her front steps. She wished she hadn't chosen today to wear her new heels and silk suit to work.

Thanks to the storm, the streetlights had come on early, and their reflection glinted off the puddle of water near her porch. As she reached the top of the stairs, a dark shape rose from the shadows.

Swallowing a scream, she clutched the railing to steady herself. Gideon Tate leaped forward and grabbed her arm to keep her from falling.

"Sorry," he said. "I didn't mean to startle you."

"What are you doing here?" she said, yanking her arm away. "We agreed to meet on Friday."

"You suggested Friday. I didn't agree to anything." His gaze traveled over her, from her now damp heels to the water spots on her blue silk skirt, and lingered on the V-neck of her white silk blouse. "I'm not a patient man."

His black slacks and black turtleneck blended with the shadows behind him, and the half-light emphasized the strong planes of his face. And the stubborn set of his jaw.

A shiver ran up her spine. It was irritation, she told herself. "How did you find out where I live?" She narrowed her eyes, ignoring the unwanted prickling along her skin. "Did Ray Dobbs tell you?"

"No. I called my office and asked them to get me the information." He opened his wallet and held it up. "I'm an assistant district attorney in Milwaukee."

She glanced at the picture of Gideon on the identification card. Damn it. The guy even took a good ID picture. "You abused your privileges, Mr. Tate."

"No, I didn't. I'm acting on behalf of a client, and I would have neglected my duty to him if I waited until Friday to talk to you."

He smiled, and uneasiness stirred. She had underestimated Gideon Tate. "What do you want?"

"What I said on the phone. To talk to you." He glanced at the house.

"Forget it," she said. "You're not coming in." She didn't let men into her house, even the handful of times she'd been on a date in the past several years. Her home was her refuge, the place she was safe. Her husband's brother was the last man she'd allow inside.

"I didn't expect you to let me in. You barely know

me." He gestured at the swing. "We can stay out here. Or we can go to that coffee shop."

"It's not open in the evening," she said. Her gaze touched the swing. She didn't want to sit with him in the semidarkness. It was too intimate. "Are you sure this can't wait until Friday?"

"No, it can't." She couldn't read his expression. "Have you eaten dinner?"

"Not yet."

"I'm hungry, and you probably are, too. I noticed a restaurant downtown. How about we get something to eat while we talk?"

"Not at the Lazy Susan," she said automatically, then mentally kicked herself. She should have just said no, instead of discussing dining options with him.

"Is there something wrong with the food?"

Everyone in Spruce Lake would know she'd eaten dinner with Gideon Tate by the time they got the check. "It's pretty busy in the evening. There's a place outside of town that's quieter."

"Sounds good."

Zoe wanted nothing to do with Gideon. But she was going to have to deal with him until the situation with Wallace was resolved. She might as well get it over with.

Gideon would be a distraction she couldn't afford.

And she refused to examine why she was afraid he'd become one.

"You can follow me in your car," she said.

"I don't have my car. I walked over here."

The sky darkened as the second wave of the storm approached and thunder rumbled again. Closer. Gideon stood patiently in front of her, and she hesitated. Her car was small. If she drove, he'd be too close.

Wallace's house was a mile away. He'd get soaked if he went back for his vehicle.

Jiggling her keys in her hand, glancing at the threatening clouds above them, she said, "I'll drive."

The sky opened as she backed into the street. Rain drummed on the roof and made the cramped space seem even smaller. The scent of his leather jacket and the crisp, clean tang of soap filled the car, mixing with the smell of the rain. When she found herself inhaling deeply, she reached blindly for the gearshift. Her fingers brushed his leg, which was jammed against the lever.

She froze for a moment, and so did he. Then he jerked his leg away as she shifted into Drive. The car bucked and the wheels spun on the wet street.

"Driving in a storm can be unnerving," he said, no inflection in his voice.

So was sitting in a tiny car with her husband's brother right next to her. A man she was suddenly too aware of. "I've driven in plenty of storms, Mr. Tate."

He glanced over at her. "Why don't you call me Gideon? It's friendlier than Mr. Tate."

"Maybe I don't want to be friendly." Oh, great. Now she sounded like a petulant child. "I mean, under the circumstances, maybe some formality between us is good."

"What circumstances would those be?"

"The situation with your father."

"I told you this had nothing to do with my father."

He was staring out the windshield into the rain and she couldn't see his expression. She wanted to be able to watch his face when he told her what was going on, so she didn't pursue the subject. Instead, she let the silence grow between them.

He gave no indication that he cared.

Apparently Gideon was comfortable with silence.

They finally reached the Pasta Bowl and dashed through the rain to the door. They ordered their drinks and meal, and she waited for her iced tea to arrive before asking, "What's this about, Mr. Tate?"

He took a swallow of his beer. "I'm representing Dave Johnson and I need to speak to his wife, Barb. She's in your shelter."

CHAPTER FIVE

"EXCUSE ME?" Zoe set her glass of tea down sharply. "What do you mean, you represent Dave Johnson?"

"Just what I said. I'll be defending Dave against the charges of spousal abuse, so I'd like to talk to his wife."

"You can talk to her in court." Zoe was so furious she could barely speak. "What's Dave trying to pull?"

Gideon's expression hardened. "My client wants to know the exact same thing about Barb. What's her scheme?"

"She's trying to protect herself," Zoe said hotly. "That's her 'scheme.' That's why she's at the shelter."

"Dave said he didn't touch her. That he's never hit her in their seven years of marriage. I believe him."

"Of course you do," she said scornfully. "Because you know everything there is to know about a man you met yesterday."

"I've known Dave almost my whole life," he said. Gideon's eyes glinted. "He was my brother's best friend."

"I'm well aware of that." It was one of the reasons she'd believed Barb. "But since you never saw your brother, how could you possibly know so much about Dave?" Hearing her voice rise, Zoe took a deep calming breath. She needed to think, instead of react. There were only three or four other couples in the restaurant, but she didn't want to draw their attention. "Or are you helping him to punish me?" she asked.

"Don't flatter yourself," he said. "This isn't about you."

"Isn't it? The fact that you're suddenly defending your brother's best friend who's been accused of beating his wife is completely coincidental?"

"Derrick has nothing to do with this," he said, but she saw a telltale flicker in his eyes. "I lived here until I was twelve, and I knew Dave pretty well."

"So you're basing your defense of Dave on a kid you knew twenty years ago?"

"I ran into him again in college. That's where he met Barb. I got to know her there, too." He leaned forward, and his scent drifted over her. "Does Barb Johnson strike you as the type of woman who's abused?"

"There is no 'type' of woman who's abused," she said automatically, determined not to back down. But he was in her space, and it made her uncomfortable. She hated him being this close.

She didn't tell him that she'd been surprised when Barb showed up at her door. That her intuition had nudged her to probe Barb's story. But she'd ignored her discomfort in the face of the woman's obvious distress. And her bruises.

"Barb was an assertive, confident woman when I knew them in college," he said bluntly. "I have a hard time believing she changed that much."

"She came to me with bruises. She said she got them from her husband. I don't give my clients the third degree. By the time they get to Safe Harbor, they've already been traumatized enough."

"You accept everything they say as gospel truth."

Zoe sighed. "Mr. Tate, when a woman is desperate

enough to come to a shelter, she's usually been to the emergency room more than once. Her husband has been arrested for domestic violence more than once. There's no question that she's telling the truth."

"Barb didn't see a doctor about injuries. She didn't call the police. So why did you believe her?"

Because Barb had been terrified her husband would find her. Jumpy. Shaking like a leaf. "Her demeanor was typical of an abused woman."

"In other words, you didn't ask her any questions."

"No. I didn't think it was necessary." Zoe wasn't used to being on the defensive about her work, and she didn't like it. "The police came to interview her," she said. "They thought she was telling the truth."

He nodded. "So the police are always right."

"Of course not," she said impatiently. "But my first concern is taking care of the women who need help. The questions can wait until they're safe." It was time to take back control of this conversation. "It's obvious you're an attorney, Mr. Tate. You twist words very well."

"One of my many talents," he agreed.

The waitress delivered their meals and Zoe picked at her spinach lasagna. "I'm surprised you're defending Dave Johnson," she said. "Being a prosecutor, I would have thought you'd be on my side of this issue."

"I usually am," he said, cutting into his chicken piccata. "But I believe Dave, so we'll have to agree to disagree." He raised one eyebrow. "How about those Packers?"

"That's it?" she asked, incredulous. "You're just giving up? You're not going to try to browbeat me into letting you talk to Barb?"

"Would it help?"

"Of course not."

"Then why would I waste my time?" He drank some beer. "I know a lost cause when I see it."

His gaze made her stomach flutter, and that irritated her. "I'm glad you're going to be reasonable."

"That depends on what you mean by reasonable. I suspect it doesn't match my definition."

"No kidding." She sipped her iced tea, glad she'd decided against a glass of wine. She needed all her wits to deal with Gideon.

"We're not on opposite sides here," he said. "You want justice. So do I."

"We have different versions of justice. I want men to be accountable for their actions. Apparently you don't."

"I'm all for accountability," he said. "On both sides. I'm not arguing about that."

"Just about Barb Johnson."

He shrugged. "You need to be more objective. Maybe the fact that Dave was Derrick's friend is coloring your decisions about Barb. Maybe you're not the best person to deal with Barb and Dave." He ate another piece of chicken. "Maybe you're not the best person to be running a shelter."

"I'm exactly the right person to be running a shelter. I know what it's like to feel helpless and have no options. To be isolated and alone and scared." She gave him a level look. "When I talk to my clients, they know I've stood in their shoes." She'd eaten half of her lasagna and hadn't tasted a bite of it. She pushed it away. "That shelter is making a difference in people's lives."

"It's certainly making a difference in Dave Johnson's life."

Gideon Tate was quick. He'd be a formidable opponent in a courtroom. She would make sure Barb was prepared to face him. "I'd say Dave did that all by himself."

"We'll see, won't we?"

She poked at her salad in an uncomfortable silence. Then Gideon said, "Do your sisters work at your shelter?"

"No, they don't. Why would you think that?"

"You seemed inseparable when you were kids. I remember seeing you around town with your father, the three of you dressed in the same outfits."

"How did you even remember I have sisters?"

"Are you kidding? You were famous in Spruce Lake."

Gideon thought they were famous. That would have made her father very happy. "I'm sure we were really cute in our matching dresses and shoes," she said, trying to keep her voice light. She and her sisters had rebelled when they'd turned eight and refused to dress alike. Their father's resulting tantrum had been frightening.

Gideon set his fork down. "I suppose you were. I was eleven or twelve. I thought you guys looked like a freak show. One of you was always herding the other two along."

"That would have been me," she said woodenly. A freak show. That was exactly what they'd been.

"Yeah? You didn't like being a triplet?"

"I loved being a triplet. Still do." She moved the lasagna around on her plate. "I just don't like being a curiosity."

"You must be used to it. You went from being the center of attention as a kid to the center of attention as an adult," he said, his voice neutral.

She placed her fork carefully on her plate. "Are you referring to your brother's death?"

"My brother's murder, you mean?"

"It's not murder if it's self-defense," she said calmly. "And it was."

"You told a good story, that's for sure."

"The jury believed me."

"Your attorney was clever," he said, his voice expressionless. "She knew how to play to them. Both of you did."

He thought she'd been playing to the jury at her trial? She'd been one step away from catatonic after sitting in jail for almost nine months. "You know nothing about me, Mr. Tate."

"I know all I need to know."

She shouldn't ask. It would only make her mad. But she heard herself say, "And that would be?"

"You killed my brother and got off scot-free. That tells me the kind of woman you are."

"I'll tell you what kind of woman I am." She signaled for the check. "I'm the kind of woman who wants to live. If I hadn't killed Derrick, he would have killed me."

When the waitress arrived with the check, Gideon plucked the folder out of the woman's hand before she put it on the table.

"You're not paying for my dinner, Gideon," Zoe said. *She'd called him Gideon. Damn it.* She was determined to keep this businesslike.

"I was the one who invited you." He studied the bill, holding the folder just out of her reach.

"This is business," she said, placing enough money on the table to cover her meal and the tip.

He finally set the check down and added his own cash to hers. "Don't want to take gifts from the enemy?"

"Are you my enemy?" She managed to keep her voice casually amused, but his words stung.

"What do you think?"

"I think attorneys who let their cases get personal aren't very good attorneys."

"You don't think I'd take it personally that you killed my brother?"

"I thought we were talking about Dave and Barb Johnson's case," she said smoothly.

His eyes locked on hers. "Quick as well as smart," he murmured.

His eyes were golden brown, she realized. They caught the light from the candle on the table and reflected it back at her. When she realized she was staring, heat crept up her cheeks. "You're not going to flatter me into getting what you want," she said.

He slid his wallet into his pocket. "And what would that be?" he asked.

"I'm not going to let you talk to Barb."

"I guess I'll have to figure out another way around your defenses," he said lightly. Her stomach swooped when his gaze lingered on her mouth.

Was he *flirting* with her? And was she responding? She shoved away from the table. "We're done here." The table wobbled when she bumped it with her thighs. "Let's go." What was wrong with her? This was Derrick's *brother,* for heaven's sake. A *Tate.*

He followed as she stalked out to her car. Neither said a word on the drive into town. The storm had passed, but it was still drizzling. "Where would you like me to drop you off?" she said, her voice frosty.

"Anywhere is fine," he said.

"I'm not going to make you walk in the rain." Even though she'd like to stop and let him out right now. She wanted him out of her space. Out of her car, where she could feel the heat of his arm close to hers, smell his already too-familiar scent.

"You're very considerate." His voice was low and intimate in the tiny space of the car. Seductive.

Stop that. "Did you say you're staying at your father's house?"

"Yes. Thanks." The intimacy disappeared from his voice, leaving it cool and distant. She glanced at him out of the corner of her eye. His mouth was tight and he stared straight ahead.

A few minutes later she swung into Wallace's driveway. No lights were on and the draperies on the first floor were closed. The bushes across the front of the house were overgrown, hanging into the driveway and partially blocking the walk to the front door. Branches scraped against the car door as she rolled to a stop.

She glanced at the shrubs pressing against the car door. "It's a narrow driveway."

"I don't mind close quarters. Even if there's something prickly on the other side." His gaze swept over her. "In fact, sometimes prickly is good. Sometimes prickly protects a sweet center."

"I doubt there's anything sweet inside those bushes."

"You never know."

The currents swirling through the car were disturbing. "I never asked how your father was doing," she said, trying to dispel them.

He shrugged. "Better. Yesterday the doctors injected a drug into the clot that caused the stroke, and he had some movement in his left arm and leg this morning. He's still not talking very well, but I can understand a few words."

"I'm glad."

"Why?" he said. "It sounds as if he's been a thorn in your side for a long time."

"That doesn't mean I want him to be disabled," she said. "I want him out of my hair. But I'd never wish a stroke on anyone."

He reached for the door handle. "It's too bad we're on opposite sides, Zoe," he murmured.

"Why is that?"

"You're an interesting woman." He smiled. "Very controlled. It makes me wonder what's beneath that cool, competent exterior."

"More of the same," she said briskly.

"Really?" The amber lights in his brown eyes gleamed. "Might be fun to see if that's true." Without waiting for an answer, he stepped out of the car.

And pushed through the bushes as though they weren't there.

"HE WAS FLIRTING with me!" Zoe said as she sat at the kitchen table with her sisters in their father's house. It was the morning after her dinner with Gideon, and the three of them were supposed to be sorting photographs they'd found in the attic, but the boxes of pictures lay ignored on the table. "When I dropped him off at home. Like we were on a date or something."

Bree shoved her long hair behind her ears. "You slugged him, didn't you?"

Zoe choked out a laugh. "Bree, I run a women's shelter. To help women who are victims of violence. I don't hit people."

"Were you flirting with him, too?" Fiona asked, narrowing her eyes.

"Of course not." The memory of how she'd reacted

to Gideon made her angry and embarrassed. "Don't you think I have more sense than that?"

"I hope you do." Fiona turned to Bree. "You keep an eye on her while I'm in New York. And this guy, too."

"She never listens to me," Bree said. "You better stick around if you want to save Zoe from herself."

"I'm right here, guys," Zoe reminded them. "And I don't need saving. You think I'd get involved with a Tate again?"

"We know how it works. It starts with flirting," Bree said darkly. "He's gorgeous and sexy and you're feeling that *zing,* but you don't want to get involved. You think you're safe. The next thing you know, you've got your tongue down his throat and his hands are on your butt."

How did Bree know Gideon was gorgeous and sexy? "Gideon Tate did not have his hands on my butt. And I most definitely didn't have my tongue down his throat," Zoe said. But the idea made her shiver.

"I'm just saying," Bree retorted. "Watch yourself, Zo."

"Don't worry," Zoe answered. "I'm immune to all Tates." She picked up a handful of photos, determined to distract her sisters. "Here's one of us with Mom."

The picture showed their mother smiling, her arms draped over all three girls' shoulders. They were eight years old, and Bree and Fiona leaned into their mother. Fiona wore red cowboy boots and a blue-and-green-striped dress. Bree wore one of her dance costumes. Zoe stood next to Fiona, holding her sister's hand, wearing jeans and a T-shirt. Their mother had always called Zoe and Fiona her matched set.

"I remember those boots, Fee," Bree said. "You wouldn't wear anything else for months."

Fiona studied the picture for a moment, then placed it facedown on the table. "Dad threw them away. He said I'd outgrown them."

An hour later, they'd sorted through most of the pictures, discarding any of people they couldn't identify. Zoe picked up the last envelope and slid out the photos. They were faded and well-thumbed. Her hand stilled.

"Look at these," she said.

They were of three tiny babies, all sleeping in the same crib. They'd heard the story often enough, about how their parents could only afford one crib at first, and all of them had slept together.

Zoe wore a blue sleeper, Bree a green one and Fiona yellow. Their arms and legs were tangled together, and if it hadn't been for the color differences, it would have been hard to tell which arm or leg belonged to which girl. Zoe's throat tightened as she looked at them. They'd been so close as young children. Three parts of a whole.

Now they were together again in their childhood house, but they were no longer connected.

They were three individuals sharing an uneasy truce.

"At least they didn't put me in pink," Zoe muttered as she handed the pictures to her sisters.

Fiona stared at the photos for a long moment, then passed them to Bree and stood up abruptly. "I need to arrange for a limo. I'm heading back to New York tonight."

"I thought you had a few more days before you had to leave," Bree said.

"Change of plans."

"I'll take you to the airport, Fee," Zoe said.

"We'll all go," Bree added.

Fiona shook her head. "Thanks, but I have work to do on the way. A limo would be better."

"You can work in the car," Zoe said. "We'd get to spend a little time together."

"Stop trying to organize us, Zoe," Fiona said. "I'll take a limo. I can't deal with all this togetherness, okay? I need a little space."

Fiona hurried out of the kitchen and clattered up the stairs. Zoe and Bree sat frozen at the table, listening to her retreat.

Fiona's bedroom door clicked shut with a deafening finality.

CHAPTER SIX

GIDEON WALKED into his father's hospital room the next afternoon and found Wallace sitting in a chair with a young woman supporting his left arm. She looked up at him.

"Hi," she said cheerfully. "Are you related to Wallace?"

"I'm Gideon Tate. His son." Gideon had introduced himself frequently in the past few days as Wallace's son, but the words still felt awkward on his tongue.

Wallace clearly heard his discomfort, because he glared at Gideon. He jerked away from the woman holding him up, but then began to topple to the side. She had to steady him.

Pity stirred in Gideon. His father was a proud man. It must be devastating for him to be helpless.

"Hi, Dad," he said, trying to sound cheerful. "You're out of bed. That's great. Dr. Trenton said yesterday's surgery would help."

"I'm Chris, the physical therapist," the young woman said. "I'll be working with your father twice a day. Right now we're practicing sitting up, aren't we, Wallace?"

"I am," his father managed to say, and Gideon smiled at the therapist.

"I guess he doesn't like the royal 'we,'" he said. "My father isn't going to be the easiest patient you've ever had."

Wallace tried to speak, but the words were garbled.

Gideon got the message, though. His father didn't want him there.

That was fine, because Gideon didn't want to be there. He'd rather be in Milwaukee, doing his job. Living his life.

"I've had tough patients before," Chris said, turning back to Wallace. "We'll get along just fine. He wants to be independent, don't you, Wallace?"

Gideon had no trouble reading the anger and fear in his father's eyes as the old man looked from him to Chris. Without thinking, Gideon took his father's right hand, the one unaffected by his stroke. Wallace's fingers curled around his.

Gideon stared down at their joined hands. He hadn't touched his father in years. Now he'd taken his hand for the second time in two days. And the old man had let him.

He must be getting soft.

Gideon released Wallace and patted his knee. "Looks like you need to get back to your therapy, Dad. I don't want to interrupt. I'll be back this afternoon."

Gideon watched his father as Chris began talking to him again. He had no idea how to communicate with the man. No idea how to help him. He wasn't sure if his presence was good for his father or making the situation worse.

It didn't matter. Being in Spruce Lake wasn't a choice. It was a duty. He wasn't going anywhere.

GIDEON SHIFTED in the hideously uncomfortable chair in the tiny lounge at the end of the corridor, trying to focus on the newspaper. Nothing happened quickly in a hospital. He felt as if he'd been waiting for his father's doctor to come by for hours.

He saw Zoe McInnes out of the corner of his eye, and

he lowered the paper. She was walking down the corridor, dressed in another killer suit. This one was dark green, and the heels she wore made her legs look a mile long.

All he could see was her straight back, the curve of her rear end, her dark hair. And those legs. How had he known immediately it was Zoe?

The instant recognition made him uneasy. He'd flirted with her last night, but he'd only been poking a little bit, trying to gauge her reactions. Trying to figure her out.

There was no way he'd flirt with Zoe and actually mean it.

He wanted to punish her, not get involved with her. He wanted to make her pay for what she'd done to his brother. And now his father.

A few minutes later, as he was wandering down to ask the nurses if they'd heard from Dr. Trenton, he saw Zoe in a patient's room. She was sitting next to a woman in a hospital bed, patting the woman's hand. A hand sticking out of a cast. A uniformed police officer sat on the other side of the bed, scribbling on a notepad.

Gideon slowed, staring at Zoe. What was she doing? She brushed the woman's hair out of her face and smiled. The woman on the bed relaxed and said something to the police officer.

Zoe looked up and saw him. She stilled, then her cheeks colored and she turned back to the woman in the bed. He watched her for a moment longer, then continued on to the nurses' station.

He smiled politely at one of the nurses and asked when the doctor was expected, telling himself to focus on his father's condition. But Zoe's face, her eyes cool and steady but her cheeks pink, kept intruding.

Zoe was still in the woman's room when Gideon retreated to the lounge. He picked up his paper and began to read again, but he knew immediately when Zoe left the room. She headed down the hall in his direction but slowed when she saw him watching her.

For a moment he thought she was going to ignore him and keep going, but at the last second she stepped into the lounge.

"Hello, Gideon. How's your father this morning?"

She was polite and composed. But she'd called him Gideon. He stood up. "Better." He gestured to one of the torturous chairs. "Have a seat?"

She hesitated, and he found himself saying, "I don't bite. At least not in public."

"Is that right?" She raised her eyebrows as she settled into one of the chairs. "I wasn't worried. I know how to bite back."

"I'll keep that in mind." An unexpected sizzle hit low in his belly. "What are you doing at the hospital?"

Her expression hardened. "One of my clients thought her husband had changed, so she went back to him. She ended up in the hospital, and this time she's pressing charges. I came by to hold her hand while she gave the police her statement."

"Literally, it looked like," he said.

"Whatever it takes to keep them safe."

"Like you're keeping Barb safe from Dave."

"Exactly."

"Do you rehearse *their* stories with them, as well?"

Her mouth tightened. "I rehearsed nothing with Barb. I don't have to coach these women. Their stories are already unbearable."

"Has Barb talked to an attorney?" he asked.

"Yes. A woman came by yesterday."

"Someone local?"

Zoe's eyes flickered. "No. She was from Green Bay. I didn't know her."

"There are no good attorneys in Spruce Lake?" He edged closer, deliberately crowding her personal space. He'd honed his courtroom tactics from years of experience, and they worked in real life, as well.

"Of course there are." She crossed her legs and smoothed her skirt, acknowledging his strategy. Telling him she didn't feel at all intimidated. "But some people feel more comfortable with a stranger. I assume Barb's one of them."

"I'll want the name of her attorney," he said.

"I'll need to get back to you on that. I don't have her name and phone number with me." The look she gave him assured him she'd stall as long as possible.

"Why did Dobbs arrest you the day my father had his stroke?"

She looked startled, as if surprised he'd question Dobbs's authority. Then she shrugged. "It was a power play," she said. "That's all."

"A power play? Over what?"

"Dobbs is retiring from the police department soon, and he wants a job on the college security force. He thinks Wallace can get it for him. So he's Wallace's best friend."

"He couldn't arrest you just because he's Wallace's friend."

"He said I pushed Wallace down."

"Did you?" he asked sharply.

"Of course not. As much as I might have been tempted, I don't assault old men."

"Then Dobbs made it up."

She adjusted her skirt. "Your father was shaking his finger in my face. That…bothers me. I pushed his finger away."

"And pushed him down in the process?"

"I didn't make your father have a stroke, Gideon. And that's why he fell."

"Obviously the police don't think so."

"No one on the police force thinks it was my fault, including Ray Dobbs. But he was delighted to have an excuse to harass me. To lock me up again." Her face tensed and she began to stand up.

He didn't want her to leave. Because he wanted to ferret out the truth, he told himself. That was the only reason. "You didn't go to prison for killing my brother."

"I spent nine months in jail before the trial," she retorted. "Wallace and his attorney convinced the judge I was a risk and I was refused bail."

Gideon frowned. He hadn't known that. Women involved in domestic cases were rarely denied bail.

"So Dobbs has a grudge against you."

"He's vindictive, and he's always resented me. He thinks I got away with murder." She gave him a cool look. "Just like you do."

It was tough to rattle her, and he needed to get inside her defenses. To make her angry. Maybe then he'd see the real Zoe McInnes, the woman who killed his brother.

Dr. Trenton strolled into the waiting room before he could respond to Zoe. "Good morning, Mr. Tate." He nodded to Zoe. "Hey, Zoe." He couldn't hide the curiosity in his eyes, but he said to Gideon, "I just saw your father. He's looking better this morning. Injecting the drug directly into the clot helped."

"I was surprised he was sitting up."

"He's got a long road ahead of him. I'm going to keep him in the hospital for several more days at least. But eventually he'll need to go to a rehab center. There are some in Green Bay I can recommend." He stuck the chart he was holding under his arm. "The good news is, I think he's going to recover most of his function. It will just take a while."

"Thanks, Doc," Gideon said, shaking his hand. "That's good to know."

The doctor flicked another inquisitive glance at Zoe, then left the room.

Zoe stood up. "On that note, I'd better get going."

"What note?" Gideon stood, too.

She rolled her eyes. "Luke Trenton is a great doctor, but he's also a gossip. If I stay much longer, half the hospital staff is going to wander by, just to see me talking to Derrick's brother."

"So what?"

"You've obviously never had people stare at you when you walk down the street." Her knuckles whitened on the strap of her purse. "I've been there and done that and don't want to do it again." She walked out the door, saying over her shoulder, "Later, Gideon."

Well, at least they were past Mr. Tate, he thought as he watched her hips sway in the tight green skirt. If she was going to let her guard down, she first had to trust him enough to call him by name.

He mulled over what she'd said as she turned the corner and disappeared. So the police chief had it in for her. He knew a lot of police officers, and most of them were professional and good at their jobs. Dobbs must have a reason for going after Zoe.

Maybe he should have a talk with him.

* * *

"Is CHIEF DOBBS in?" Gideon asked the clerk at the front desk of the small Spruce Lake police station.

"Let me check. Can I give him your name?"

"Gideon Tate. Wallace's son."

The young woman picked up the phone. After a brief conversation, she nodded at Gideon. "Go on back. His office is at the end of the hall."

Ray Dobbs was sitting back in his chair when Gideon walked in. He jumped up and reached across the desk to shake his hand. "Good to see you, Gideon. How's your father doing?"

"Better," Gideon replied. "The doctor's optimistic."

"That's great. Good news." Dobbs gestured to a chair and sat down himself. "What can I do for you?"

"I want to talk to you about Zoe McInnes."

The smile disappeared from Dobbs's face. "I'm working on it. I'm talking to the DA about charging her with assault. She pushed your father, you know."

"The DA is going to let you charge her?" Gideon asked, disbelieving. "Even though my father had a stroke?"

Dobbs shrugged. "He hasn't signed off on it yet. But he'll come around. He owes me one."

"Zoe seems to think you hold a grudge against her."

Dobbs's friendliness disappeared. "She committed murder and got away with it. Of course I hold a grudge." Dobbs looked him up and down. "Are you taking her side? I'd think you'd hold a grudge, too. Just like your daddy."

"I'm not my father," Gideon said coldly. "But I would like more information. What evidence didn't come out at her trial?"

"Nothing was held back, as far as I know. Doesn't matter. I got all I needed." Dobbs pointed his index finger at Gideon and mimed shooting him. "She put a bullet through your brother's heart, using his own gun. She never denied it."

"And Wallace?"

"She shoved him. That's assault."

"She claims she just pushed his finger out of her face. Did you talk to any of the witnesses at the coffee shop?

"You *are* taking her side. And now you're telling me how to do my job?" Dobbs's chair creaked as he shifted.

"No. I'm asking *if* you've done your job. Because if she's responsible for my father's stroke, I don't want her to wriggle out of it again."

Dobbs stared at him for a long moment, his expression flat and hard, and Gideon realized Dobbs would be a powerful enemy. "You're a cocky son of a bitch, aren't you? Wallace told me he'd disowned you," Dobbs said. "Now I know why."

Gideon stood up. "I'm just looking for information. I want to see an airtight case against her this time."

"I don't need some punk from out of town telling me how to do my job," Dobbs said.

"Are you sure?" He held Dobbs's gaze and felt a jolt of satisfaction when Dobbs looked away first. "I want her to pay as much as anyone. But if you pursue Zoe without the evidence to back you up, you're going to embarrass yourself and the police force, not to mention Wallace," Gideon said coldly. "And he's not going to associate with people who embarrass him."

He walked out of the office without waiting for an answer.

ZOE WAS ON THE PHONE with Helen Cherney, talking to her about the woman Jamie Evans had brought to Safe Harbor the day before, when the shelter's doorbell rang.

She glanced out the window and saw a Spruce Lake police car sitting at the curb.

"I have to go, Helen. The police are here. If it's Jamie, I'll give him your love." She hung up, laughing, as her normally poised attorney sputtered into the phone.

Her smile disappeared when she looked through the peephole and saw Ray Dobbs on the porch. She reluctantly opened the door. "Chief Dobbs. What can I do for you?"

"You think you're pretty clever, don't you, Zoe? Sending Wallace's son to pump me for information. To threaten me." His eyes were cold and flat. Merciless.

Cop's eyes.

She'd never thought of Dobbs as a real cop. He was a cartoon figure, a blowhard whose allegiance to Wallace made her dismiss him as the old man's lapdog. His flunky.

But as she stared at him standing on the porch, uneasiness snaked down her spine. There was menace in his gaze, and hatred.

A rottweiler disguised as a lapdog.

"I have no idea what you're talking about," she managed to say.

His expression hardened. "Is that right?" he said softly. "You didn't tell Tate to come talk to me about the evidence against you? He thought of that all by himself?"

"I barely know Gideon Tate."

"You were real cozy with him at dinner last night. For someone you barely know."

She was stunned that he'd found out about their dinner. Uneasiness morphed into fear. "You were spying on me?"

"I keep track of troublemakers." He smiled, and the final traces of the buffoon disappeared, leaving a bully, confident in his power and control. "In case they cause problems. And you are causing problems, Zoe." He nodded slowly. "I'll be keeping a real close eye on you. And those sisters of yours and that kid. They look like troublemakers, too."

Dobbs walked down the sidewalk and climbed into his cruiser without looking back. Wrapping her arms around herself, Zoe shivered as he drove away.

CHAPTER SEVEN

THE GROCERY STORE wasn't usually this crowded on Friday evening, but the Quik Pik was trying to modernize and had begun selling ready-made meals. Zoe waved to two women who'd volunteered at her shelter as she maneuvered her cart past the deli and into the produce department.

She wanted to spend time with Bree and Charlie, so the three of them were going to fix a meal together. Just like a normal family. Maybe she and Bree could have a conversation that didn't end in an argument.

Zoe tossed a head of lettuce into her cart, then a bag of tomatoes and a bunch of carrots. Salad would go with just about anything Bree and Charlie picked out in the meat department. Zoe was sorting through the green peppers when she glanced over at the bakery.

Her hand tightened on the pepper she held. Gideon Tate was pushing a cart and studying the display of bread. The anger that had been simmering since Chief Dobbs's visit bubbled up and overflowed.

By the time she threaded her way through the other shoppers, Gideon had disappeared around the corner. Finally she spotted him in front of the cheese case.

As she wove through the people crowding the aisle, she murmured, "Hey, Jilly, pardon me. Excuse me,

Larry." Before she could reach Gideon, however, Bree stepped in front of the cart and dropped in a shrink-wrapped chicken.

"Found just the thing for dinner," Bree said with satisfaction. "I have this great recipe for roasted chicken."

"Get out of the way, Bree," Zoe said. "I have to catch him."

"Who?" Bree turned and peered down the aisle.

"Gideon Tate."

Bree grabbed the cart. "What for?"

"I'll tell you later." Zoe swerved around her sister, but Gideon had disappeared again. "Damn it, Bree." She dumped the green pepper in the cart. "You made me lose him."

"What's wrong with you?" Bree said in a low voice. "What's so important that you have to catch him?"

"Dobbs," Zoe said, watching to see if Gideon reappeared. "He paid me a visit this afternoon and threatened us. All of us."

"What does Gideon Tate have to do with that?"

"Gideon got him stirred up. I'm not sure what he said, but it made Dobbs mad."

Her voice had risen and Bree muttered, "Be quiet, Zoe. You're making a scene. Everyone's looking at us."

Zoe froze. Bree knew exactly how to shut her up. After enduring their father's scenes, they all lived in horror of people staring at them.

"I'm going to find him and tell him to knock it off," Zoe said, struggling to keep her voice down. "Go find Charlie so we can get out of here."

"He's talking to some friends of his from school," Bree said, glancing behind her. "There he is."

"Hey, Mom. Aunt Zo." Charlie appeared in front of

them, his hands shoved into the pockets of his baggy jeans. Watching him from the other end of the store were two children, a boy and girl. A tall blond man stood next to them at the meat counter, talking to the butcher. "Is it okay if I go over to Logan and Lindy's?"

"I don't know their parents," Bree said, turning to look at the kids. "I need to meet them first."

"That's their father, Jackson Grant," Zoe said to Bree, still trying to restrain her temper as she nodded toward the man with the children. "You must not remember— he was three years ahead of us in school." She should be grateful for the interruption, for the chance to calm down, but she didn't want to calm down. She wanted to get rid of her anger by dumping it onto Gideon.

"Yeah?" Bree said doubtfully. "Is he a responsible parent?"

"He's the veterinarian here in town," Zoe said, forcing herself to focus on her sister. "Word is he got custody of his kids a while ago. I think they're around Charlie's age."

"Twins?" Bree asked, a hint of wistfulness in her voice.

"Yes." Zoe leaned around to examine Bree's face. "Are those cow eyes for the kids or for Jackson?"

Bree glanced at Jackson, then back at Logan and Lindy. "He's not my type," she said. "But the kids sure look happy."

Unlike you and Fiona and me at that age. Bree didn't have to say the words. "Lucky them," Zoe said lightly.

"Hello, Jackson," Zoe said to the man as he approached them. "Logan, Lindy, how are you?"

The twins shrugged. "Okay."

"Okay, what?" their father prompted.

The girl rolled her eyes. "Okay, Ms. McInnes."

Bree turned to the tall blond man with a cautious smile. "I'm Bree McInnes, Charlie's mother," she said, holding out her hand.

"Jackson Grant," the man said. "We're going to have pizza and movies at our place tonight. Is it okay if Charlie joins us?"

Bree glanced at Zoe, who gave her a slight nod. From everything she knew about Jackson, he was a good father, who'd supervise the kids.

While Bree talked to Jackson, Zoe scanned the store for any sign of Gideon. He must have left. As she watched Charlie talk to the twins, renewed anger coursed through her, hot and bubbling. Dobbs had threatened her nephew.

And Gideon put him up to it.

"I'm going to pay for this stuff," Zoe said as she headed for the checkout.

Bree caught up to her as she was unloading the groceries. "Take it easy, Zo."

"I want to talk to Gideon right now and straighten this out. Maybe I can catch up with him in the parking lot." The chicken landed on the belt and rolled toward the register.

Zoe could feel Bree's stare. "Zoe! I don't believe this. You're attracted to him, aren't you?"

"To Gideon Tate?" Something fluttered in Zoe's belly. It was just anger, she told herself. "That's the most ridiculous thing I've ever heard."

"Is it?" Bree steadied the green pepper that had landed on the edge of the counter and was about to fall to the floor. "That's a lot of passion for a man you're not interested in."

"That's not passion. It's rage," Zoe said through clenched teeth.

Bree raised her eyebrows. "Really? Hard to tell the difference."

Zoe saw the amused looks from the couple behind them in line and yanked out her wallet. "Let's get out of here," she muttered to her sister.

There was no sign of Gideon in the parking lot. She and Bree were loading the groceries in the car before Zoe realized her nephew was missing.

"I told him he could have pizza with those twins and their father." Bree opened the trunk of the car and dropped in a bag. "Jackson and his kids seemed nice enough, and I couldn't say no. Charlie needs a few friends in town."

"What did you think of our vet?" Zoe asked as they drove off. "He's considered quite the hottie in some circles."

Bree shrugged. "He might be a good guy, but not for me. No *zing*, you know? I'm not interested in dating, anyway." She gave Zoe a mischievous look. "What about you? Since he's such a catch."

"Me and Jackson?" She tried to picture the veterinarian, but all she saw was Gideon's face. "I'm like you. No *zing*."

Gideon, on the other hand, had *zing*. Lots of it.

But if she tried really hard, maybe she could pretend he didn't.

"Saving yourself for Tate?" Bree said with a sly look.

"No!" Zoe said. Too vehemently.

"I guess we'll have to save the hot vet for Fiona, then," Bree said.

"You have *got* to be kidding me," Zoe said, happy Bree was off the subject of her and Gideon. "Fee and Jackson Grant? Steady, even-tempered Mr. Homebody and moody, globe-trotting Fiona?"

"He does seem steady. Fiona needs steady." Bree nodded. "Me, I'd rather have a bit more excitement in my life."

"I'll keep my eye open for exciting," Zoe said.

Bree slumped back in the seat. "Don't bother. I've had it with men. I'll concentrate on fixing up my sisters."

"You're way off base with Jackson and Fiona," Zoe said.

"What about you and Gideon Tate? I recognize that look on your face. And I'm guessing Tate has the same look." She gazed out the window, no longer laughing. "I know when men and women are interested in each other. You might say it's my area of expertise."

"Stop it, Bree! Enough with beating yourself up about the stripping. It's in the past."

"That's naive," Bree said quietly. "You know it's not."

"Have you gone over to the high school yet and checked into the substitute-teaching job?" Zoe asked after a few moments. "Bonnie won't be going back for a while."

"Not yet."

"You should do it before they find someone else."

"I'll do it when I'm ready, Zo." Bree's voice sharpened.

"You need health insurance," Zoe said as she turned into the driveway of their father's house.

"Don't you think I know that?" Bree's voice hardened. "Stop telling me what to do, Zoe. I can take care of myself. And Charlie. You worry about yourself. And whatever's going on with Gideon Tate."

Zoe grabbed the groceries, shoved them into Bree's arms and slammed the trunk of the car. "I'll do that. In fact, I'm going to take care of Gideon Tate right now."

IMAGES OF CHARLIE being manhandled by Ray Dobbs filled her mind as she drove through the twilight gloom of Spruce Lake. By the time she reached Wallace Tate's house, anger was ready to burst out of her in a toxic flood. It was one thing to make Dobbs mad at her. She could take care of herself. It was quite another to put her nephew and sisters in harm's way.

There were no outside lights on, and only a dim yellow glow from the back of the house filtered out the front windows. Was Gideon even home?

Yes. His vehicle was parked in the driveway, the juniper branches bent against its side. Slamming her car door, she marched up to the front of the house.

The doorbell chimed loudly, but a full minute passed and there was no sign of Gideon. Maybe he wasn't home, after all. She was just about to give up when she heard footsteps.

Gideon opened the door, dressed in nothing but baggy, faded basketball shorts that hung low on his hips. His chest was glistening with sweat and his left hand was enclosed in a boxing glove. He held the other glove between his body and his upper arm.

"Zoe. What are you doing here?"

His torso and arms were all lean muscle, gleaming in the dim light. Dark hair dusted his chest and arrowed down his belly, disappearing under the shorts. A drop of sweat rolled down the side of his face, and he swiped at it with the dark red glove.

When she didn't reply, he asked, "Is there something you wanted?" He kept a careful distance from her.

His words jerked her gaze away from his bare chest. Face burning, she remembered her anger. The reason she'd come to his house.

"I need to talk to you."

"Come on in." He stepped away from the door, holding it open for her.

She breathed in a hint of sweat as she moved past him, anxious to put more space between them. He pulled off the other boxing glove and tossed both of them on the old mahogany table in the hall. "Hold on a second," he said. "I'll be right back."

He ran lightly up the stairs, the muscles in his legs bunching and flexing as he disappeared. Gideon was in good shape.

Especially for a man who sat at a desk.

He came down a few moments later, wiping his face and head with a towel. When he reached the foyer, he tossed the towel over the newel post and pulled on a gray T-shirt. His dark hair stood on end, as if someone had run fingers through it.

"What can I do for you, Zoe?"

She dragged her attention away from his hair and his body and his muscular arms. *Focus, Zoe. Remember why you're here.* "What did you say to Dobbs?" she demanded.

"What do you mean?"

"Did you tell him to leave me alone?" She heard her voice rise and struggled to control it. "What did you think you were doing?"

He studied her for a moment, and she couldn't read his eyes. "I wanted to find out what evidence he had against you," he finally said. "Because I'm not sure he has anything."

He was trying to clear her name? She ignored the tiny bubble of pleasure. "Really? You thought he'd say, 'You're right, Mr. Tate. I don't have a damn thing on her. I've been hounding her for six years, but I'll stop now.' Is that what you thought he'd say?"

"I told him he needed to find some real proof."

So he wasn't defending her. He was trying to make sure Dobbs had a good case against her.

Her bubble of happiness burst.

Why should she care? She didn't like him, either. "And you figured that would work? What kind of idiot are you, anyway?"

"He's a bully, Zoe," Gideon said. He sounded calm and rational, which only infuriated her more. "You have to stand up to bullies. If you do, they back down."

"You might want to explain that to Dobbs, because he didn't get that memo," she said. "He threatened my sisters. And my nephew." Rage pumped through her, scalding hot and fueled by helplessness. After Derrick, she'd vowed never to be helpless again.

"What do you mean, he threatened them?" Gideon grabbed her arms, pulling her closer. She could see the golden glints in his eyes. "What did he say?"

She jerked away from him. "Dobbs isn't as dumb as he seems. He doesn't make overt threats. But he gets his message across." She stared at the table in the foyer, seeing the scenarios playing in her mind. "My nephew's only twelve," she said, struggling for composure. "But I'm sure Dobbs knows that."

"I'll deal with Dobbs. He won't hurt your nephew. Or anyone else."

"You don't get it, do you? He's not going to physically attack us," she said impatiently. "Even Dobbs isn't that stupid. What he'll do is pick Charlie up on suspicion of shoplifting. When he turns out not to have anything in his pockets, Dobbs will let him go. In the meantime, Charlie will be humiliated and embarrassed." She folded her arms across her chest to keep herself from grabbing and shaking him.

"He'll stop Bree for speeding if she's going one mile over the limit. He'll give Fiona a ticket for littering or jaywalking."

"Then make sure you don't do anything illegal," he said impatiently. "Don't give him any excuse."

"Have you never driven over the speed limit, Gideon?" she asked. "Crossed a street in the middle of the block because you were in a hurry? Had something fall out of your car when you opened the door?"

She almost thought she saw anger in his eyes. On her behalf?

Don't be ridiculous. His last name is Tate.

"That's what I thought," she said. "No one's perfect. If Dobbs wants to find something, he will. No matter how careful we are."

"It shouldn't be that way."

"There's a news flash. Men shouldn't beat their wives, either. But they do." She backed away. "Stay out of my life, Gideon."

"I can't do that. My client's wife is in your shelter. So we have to be in touch whether you like it or not."

"Keep it to business," she said, narrowing her eyes.

"Of course," he said smoothly. "I'm a very businesslike guy."

But the way he was looking at her had nothing to do with business. Bree had said he was attracted to her.

And she was attracted to him.

Bree didn't know what she was talking about.

"Look, Gideon. I get that you don't like me. That you think I got away with murdering your brother. But leave the rest of my family out of it. My sisters and my nephew had nothing to do with Derrick."

"You think I don't like you, Zoe?" His eyes darkened.

"Of course you don't," she said, her heart suddenly pounding. "How could you?"

"Hell if I know." He pulled her close, then his mouth came down on hers.

His lips plundered hers, moving over them as if he wanted to consume her. His hands tightened on her upper arms, drawing her against his body. His heat burned into her. So did the evidence of his arousal.

She felt herself softening, responding to him. Opening to him. She wanted to step even closer, to twine her arms around his body.

But she wouldn't give him the satisfaction of surrendering. She wouldn't let him have that kind of power over her.

So she kissed him back until she felt his anger fading, replaced with real desire. Then she broke away, trying to steady her breathing.

"Derrick tried to control me with sex, too," she said in a low voice. "It didn't work for him. And it's not going to work for you."

CHAPTER EIGHT

HE WAS GOING to go mad.

Inactivity was driving him right over the edge.

He'd had his fill of this hospital, of the smell of sickness and disinfectant, of his father's disapproval.

Gideon paced the corridor outside the room, waiting for the therapist to finish her session with Wallace. He'd spend some time with his father, wait for the doctor, then come back in the afternoon and do it all over again.

In spite of the fact that his father didn't want him to.

That was obvious from the anger in Wallace's eyes every time he looked at his son. And in the few garbled words he managed to say, "Leave me alone" were three of his favorites. "Go home" were the other two.

Why the hell was he here, anyway? He turned at the end of the corridor and headed back to his father's room just in time to see his father try to stand up while the therapist had her back turned, writing her notes.

Gideon rushed into the room and caught his father as he swayed, easing him back down onto the bed. "You can't do that by yourself yet, Dad," he said as the therapist spun around. "You still need someone to support you."

"Wallace!" the young woman cried. "You're going to hurt yourself."

It wasn't hard to read his father's expression. He hated that Gideon had to help him. He hated relying on his son.

Almost as much as Gideon hated having to do it.

But his father had no one else. Gideon couldn't walk away from his responsibility, no matter how much he wanted to.

His phone rang and he flipped it open. "Hey, Gideon." Dave's voice.

"How's it going, Dave?" he said, stepping out of the hospital room and into the corridor.

"Great! I just heard some news."

"What's that?" Gideon asked, moving into the lounge. Through its large windows the sky over Spruce Lake was leaden gray, storm clouds hovering on the horizon. "You sound pretty pumped."

"One of my friends is on the city council, and they met last night. There's been a zoning complaint against Safe Harbor Women's Shelter. Where Barb is," he added.

Gideon paced to the other side of the room. "I know what Safe Harbor is. What kind of complaint?"

"The place is zoned as a single-family home, because that's what it was when Zoe bought it. But it's sure not a single-family home anymore."

"You sound happy about that," Gideon said cautiously, puzzled by Dave's reaction.

"Of course I am. If Barb has to leave, I'll at least be able to talk to her. To find out what she's up to."

"What about all the women who need that shelter?" Gideon asked, his hand tightening on the phone. "Where are they supposed to go?"

There was a beat of silence on the other end. Then Dave said impatiently, "There must be other places."

"Who filed this complaint?"

"It was anonymous. But the zoning commission will have to deal with it."

"Thanks for letting me know," Gideon said. "I'll check it out." He shut the phone before Dave could say anything else. Before Dave could irritate him further.

Who'd do such a mean-spirited thing?

Any of the men in Spruce Lake who resented her for siding with their wives, he admitted. For helping them escape. Zoe's advocacy for battered women had no doubt made her enemies.

He was one of them, he reminded himself sharply. But the memory of how she'd felt in his arms washed over him in a rush of heat and desire. The memory that haunted him all night. And made him sleepless with remorse.

He had no idea why he'd kissed her. To put her in her place? To show her she didn't affect him at all? But she'd managed to turn the tables on him. She'd kissed him back, then walked out the door, leaving him hot and aroused and angry. He hadn't been able to think of anything else since.

He had no obligation to tell her about the zoning complaint. No obligation to help the woman who'd killed his brother.

But he knew the good that women's shelters did. He'd seen for himself how necessary they were. He'd have to tell her about the complaint.

Guilt clawed at his gut as anticipation swelled inside him. He needed to see her again. To spend more time with her. If he was honest with himself, he would admit that he was attracted to her. That he wanted her. In spite of the fact that she killed his brother.

What kind of man was he?

* * *

HE ROSE FROM Zoe's porch swing as her car zipped into the driveway that evening. He'd been waiting there for almost an hour, in the grip of his savior complex. And a desire to see her again. He moved to the top of the stairs where she'd be able to spot him clearly. He didn't want to startle her like last time.

She stared at him a moment, then turned away to gather papers and a briefcase from the passenger seat.

She stepped out of the car, flashing a long expanse of leg beneath a navy blue suit. Slamming the car door with her hip, she said, "What are you doing here?"

"Waiting for you."

"You could have called me at the shelter," she said as she started up the steps. "You have the phone number."

"That's your turf," he answered. "You're in charge there. I want a more level playing field."

"This isn't a level playing field. It's my house." She leaned against the porch column, confident and composed. "I'm in charge here, too."

Her confidence, that "I dare you to try and rattle me" attitude, made his hands itch to touch her. To see if she would respond to him again. "It's harder to brush me off if I'm standing in front of you," he said. Sure, he could have told her about the zoning complaint over the phone. But he'd given in to his need to see her, and he wasn't about to tell her that.

"Believe me, Gideon, if I don't want to talk to you, I'd have no trouble brushing you off."

"Since you haven't, I assume talking's okay."

She sighed and pushed away from the column. "Why did you come here? A phone call would have been much simpler."

"I like to talk to people in person. It's easier to read

them." He wanted to watch those blue eyes of hers when he stepped too close.

"A skill that comes in handy for a lawyer."

She practically curled her lip when she said it, and he smiled. "You say 'lawyer' as if it's something nasty you'd find on the bottom of your shoe."

Her gaze was steady. "Derrick had just passed the bar exam when he died."

"I heard that." At Derrick's trial his father had raged about Zoe destroying his son's brilliant legal career. "That doesn't make all lawyers bad news."

"I know that. I deal with them every day." She shoved the papers she still held into her briefcase. "What do you want, Gideon?"

"Would you like to sit down?" He nodded toward the white swing swaying gently in the wind. "Or we can go to dinner if you prefer."

She studied him for a moment, then sighed. "It's too windy to sit outside, and I'm not going to dinner with you. So you might as well come in the house." She unlocked the door and he followed her inside.

His first impression was of an explosion of color in an open, airy space. The couch and two chairs were blue, with multicolored throw pillows. An oriental rug in vivid blues and reds partially covered the gleaming hardwood floor, and bookshelves lined two of the walls. Framed photographs covered the end tables and balanced on the bookshelves. Children's drawings were pinned to the walls.

"I like the art," he said, looking at them.

"I do, too." Her voice had softened, and he watched as she touched one of the drawings. It showed a stick figure holding what looked like a dog.

"What's that one about?" he asked.

Her hand hovered over the picture, then fell to her side. "A little girl named Marie who stayed at the shelter. She wanted a dog more than anything. Her father told her he'd kill any animal that came into the house."

"Did she get a dog?"

Zoe nodded but continued staring at the picture. "Marie and her mother moved to Green Bay and found an apartment that allowed pets." She turned around and smiled, but her eyes were bright. "They now have the ugliest dog on the face of the earth. Sweetie Pie."

"A success for your shelter," he said.

She shrugged. "Depends how you define success. They're safe and healing. But a marriage has been destroyed and a woman and a little girl have scars that will take a long time to heal. If they ever truly will. So I'm not sure I'd call them a success."

"What do you consider a success?" he asked.

"The day I close the doors of Safe Harbor because it's not needed. And I'm afraid that's not going to happen anytime soon." She forced a smile. "Can I get you something to drink? Iced tea? Soda? A beer?"

"A beer sounds good."

"Have a seat. I'll be right back."

A few minutes later she returned to the living room, carrying a bottle of Leinenkugel and a glass of iced tea. She'd kicked off her shoes.

"Do you need a glass?" she asked.

"Heck, no. I'm a manly man. I drink my beer out of the bottle."

She glanced at his mouth, then away. "I'll make a note of that." She folded herself into one of the chairs, tucking her legs beneath her. The red of her toenails peeked out from beneath her skirt, and he had to drag his attention away from them.

She followed the direction of his gaze and stilled. Then she casually tucked her feet under her more tightly. "Okay, Gideon. What's up?"

"That's getting down to business," he said, taking a gulp of his beer.

Her eyebrows rose. "That's why you're here, isn't it? Business?"

She knew better than that. The memory of their kiss last night was in her eyes. "We'll start with business." He set the bottle on a coaster on the table. "Dave Johnson called me today. He heard that there's been a zoning complaint against your shelter."

"What?" She froze, her glass halfway to her mouth. Carefully she put it back on the table. "What do you mean, a zoning complaint?"

"Apparently your building was originally designated a single-family home. Someone is arguing that the shelter is violating the zoning regulations because it was never rezoned and it's no longer a single-family home."

Anger flashed in her eyes. "How did Dave hear that?"

"He said he has a friend on the city council."

"Dave probably called it in himself. He phoned me at the shelter a couple of times. He's really angry that I won't let him talk to Barb."

"You don't know Dave. I do, and he wouldn't play a trick like that. He knows how important that shelter is." Gideon remembered how happy Dave had sounded when he called with the news about the shelter, and doubt crowded into his mind. He shoved it away. "He's frustrated because he doesn't understand why Barb lied about being abused."

"Gideon, I've spent the last six years helping abused women and protecting them from the men in their lives. Trust me when I say Dave is perfectly capable of calling in a complaint about the shelter. Anger makes men do a lot of things they wouldn't normally do."

"Only men?" He raised his eyebrows.

"Of course not. But women in abusive relationships are always afraid. They can't afford to get mad." She took another drink of tea. "I don't believe Barb is lying."

"We disagree on Barb and Dave, but I'm not here to discuss them," he said impatiently. "I wanted to let you know about the zoning complaint. Help you try to head it off."

Zoe jumped up from the chair and moved around the living room. The subtle swish of her skirt as she walked sounded much too loud in the suddenly quiet house. "Why are you doing this, Gideon?"

"Doing what?" He stood up as she paced. She'd discarded her jacket and her arms were smooth and firm. He remembered what they felt like beneath his fingers, and he jammed his hands into his pockets.

"Warning me about the zoning complaint. Going to Dobbs to tell him to back off." She took a breath and faced him. "Are you trying to distract me from Barb's situation? Trying to worm your way into my confidence so you can figure out how to blame me for Wallace's stroke?"

"Are you always this suspicious?" he asked.

"When someone with the last name of Tate is involved, yes, I am." She began her circuit of the room again, edging closer to him with each pass. He was sure she didn't realize that. *He* was far too aware of it. Her scent drifted over him, a sweet and tart combination of flowers and citrus. "So what are you up to? What's your agenda?"

"I thought it was fairly obvious," he said, watching her move across the rug. Her toenails were a bright splash of color against the dark blue of the carpet, and she'd wrapped her arms around herself as if she was cold.

"Not to me," she said, stopping to face him. "I don't have the time or the patience to figure out devious schemes. I'm straightforward. So spell it out for me."

"Straightforward? I don't think so, Zoe," he murmured, closing his hands around her upper arms. Her skin was even smoother than he remembered. "You have all kinds of hidden, mysterious depths. You make a man want to dive in and explore them."

He drew her nearer and her eyes darkened. "You made your point last night, Gideon. You don't like me. I get it." Her words were halting, as if she was having trouble catching her breath.

"And you don't like me, either. Remember?" He swept his tongue along her lower lip, lightly tracing its outline. She was rigid in his arms, her mouth a hard line beneath his. But when he lingered at the corner of her mouth, she shuddered against him and her lips softened.

He drew her closer until her body brushed against his, then deepened the kiss. Her mouth trembled and her lips parted, and he pressed her against him.

He'd proved his point. She wanted him, too. He could stop now. He could walk out on her, like she'd done to him the night before. They'd be even.

But he couldn't force himself to let her go.

She opened her mouth to him and desire roared through his body. He tightened his hold on her. She twined her arms around his neck and made a tiny sound deep in her throat, and he forgot all about his anger. And his guilt. He slid his fingers into the silk of her hair to hold her steady and forgot every bit of his caution. She tasted like the mint in her iced tea, like every forbidden thing he'd ever wanted.

Tugging her blouse out of the waistband of her skirt, he spread his fingers over her lower back, savoring the heat of her body, the satin of her skin. Her muscles trembled beneath his hand and, lost in the feel of her, the taste, the scent, he continued to kiss her.

Her mouth moved beneath his, taking them deeper. He slid his hand around to her belly. Her skin jumped beneath his fingers, and he cupped one lush breast in his palm. She moaned as she pressed into his hand and he fumbled with the buttons of her blouse, then the clasp of her bra. When it fell open she froze, then stumbled backward, out of his arms. Away from him.

"Gideon!" She stared at him, shocked. Her mouth was still wet from his and her chest rose and fell too fast. Her cheeks were pink, and through her open blouse he could see a flush of red across her breasts. She clutched the edges of the blouse together, but her nipples were two hard points against the silky material. "What are you doing? You don't want me. And I don't want you."

"No? Sure felt like you did."

She touched her mouth, her fingers sliding across her lower lip, and he barely stopped himself from reaching for her again. His whole body throbbed.

"This was… This is…" She floundered, her cool composure gone. She was vulnerable and unsure of herself. She looked down at her blouse, then fastened the buttons with hands that shook.

He should be happy. This was what he wanted,

wasn't it? Zoe disarmed, her icy, in-control facade cracked wide open. He could walk out the door, satisfied that he'd paid her back for making him lose control last night.

He didn't want to leave. He wanted to kiss her senseless. He wanted to do a lot more than kiss her.

Guilt surged through him. This was *Zoe McInnes*. The woman who'd killed his brother. And no woman had ever gotten him so hard, so fast.

"A mistake," he said, his voice flat. "On both our parts."

She swallowed slowly, then pulled herself together as he watched. "You're right," she said. Her tightly furled nipples disagreed. "I don't know what I was thinking."

He knew exactly what *he'd* been thinking. And he could take a good guess at what was in her mind, too. The flush still hadn't faded from her cheeks. Or her chest. "I guess we both have some issues to work out," he said.

"There are no issues. There won't be any more kissing. Or touching." She grabbed her iced tea and took a long drink. "We'll just pretend this didn't happen."

"Really? You can forget about this? I'm not sure I can."

She glanced down at his crotch. "Go away, Gideon." She strode to the front door and opened it, clutching the handle. "Thank you for the warning about the zoning complaint. I'll get my lawyer on top of it right away."

"Always good to be on top of things." He leaned in to kiss her. Just to see what she'd do. She shoved him away.

"Don't do that again, Gideon."

He'd rattled her and he liked that. Liked seeing her lose control. "You sure that's what you want, Zoe?" he asked as he stepped outside. "Sure you want to forget what happened here?"

She shut the door a little too hard behind him.

CHAPTER NINE

"WHY DIDN'T WE do this right after Dad's funeral?" Bree's voice sounded as if it were coming from the end of a tunnel.

"Hmm?" Zoe jerked her attention away from the memories of Gideon and what had happened the night before. "What did you say, Bree?"

"I said why didn't we sort his stuff out before this?" Bree stuck her head out of the closet, then marched over to her. "What are you doing, Zoe? You're the one who wanted to tackle Dad's bedroom today."

Zoe looked at the box on the bed, which was empty. She was supposed to be filling it with the clothes in the dresser, she remembered guiltily.

"Sorry, Bree." Zoe stood up and opened a drawer, grabbing a handful of her father's T-shirts. "Daydreaming, I guess."

"So why *didn't* we clean out his room when we were here for the funeral?"

"You and Fiona couldn't stick around, remember?" Zoe threw a pair of socks into the box. They bounced out and onto the floor. Her sisters had fled Spruce Lake like their hair was on fire after their father's funeral. She'd resented the implied assumption that, since she lived in Spruce Lake, she could take care of cleaning out the house. "I thought we should go through his stuff together before we gave any of it away."

Bree narrowed her eyes. "Then why aren't we waiting for Fiona to come back?"

"Because who knows when that'll be?" Zoe said impatiently. "At least there are two of us. If we see anything she might want, we can set it aside for her."

"Fee's not going to want anything of Dad's," Bree said. She turned abruptly and headed back into the closet. Her voice was muffled. "Be serious, Zo."

"You never know," Zoe said. She pulled open another drawer and found his sweaters. The blue-and-yellow argyle on top had been one of his favorites. He'd worn it on Saturdays, when he'd taken his girls into town. She stared at it for a moment, then yanked out the drawer and dumped the contents into the box.

"Did he really need all these?" Bree said. She sneezed as she walked out of the closet with an armful of dusty suits on hangers.

"They were part of his image," Zoe said without looking up. "Important men dress up for work every day."

"I'll bet there wasn't one other professor in the English department who was this formal," Bree said, tossing the suits on the bed.

"Exactly why he wore them," Zoe said. "They made him stand out."

Bree sat on the bed and watched as Zoe haphazardly stuffed their father's casual shirts into the box. "What's wrong, Zo?" she asked quietly. "You've been distracted and cranky all morning, and now you're not even bothering to fold anything. What's going on?"

Zoe's hands stilled on the green polo shirt she held,

then she folded it carefully before adding it to the others. "Nothing. I'm fine."

Bree held her gaze. "You don't act like you're fine."

Zoe reached for another top, then impulsively turned to Bree. "You're right. I have been distracted. Something happened last night."

Bree cocked her head. "You want to talk about it?"

"You want to listen?"

"Of course I do," Bree said. She stood up. "Let's take a break and have some iced tea. It's warm for April. We can sit on the back steps like we used to do with Mom."

They headed downstairs, poured the drinks and walked out the door. The sun was bright and the air smelled like damp earth and flowers poised to spring to life. The dark-blue-painted steps felt hot when Zoe sat down.

"So what's up?" Bree asked.

Zoe turned the glass in her hand. "Gideon Tate came over to my house last night."

"What for?" Bree asked, scowling.

"He told me that someone had reported the shelter to the zoning commission. They said it violated regulations because it wasn't a single family house."

"What?" Bree spun to face her, practically quivering with indignation. "Someone's trying to cause trouble for the shelter?" She frowned at Zoe. "Gideon was probably the one who reported you."

"Then why would he have said anything about it to me?"

"Maybe he was afraid you'd find out and he figured you wouldn't suspect him if he told you first."

Zoe nudged at a curl of peeling paint with the toe of her shoe. "I don't think it was Gideon."

"Are you sure?" Bree, sitting next to her, leaned over

so she could see Zoe's face. "He's a Tate. That's what they do—they harass you."

"Not this Tate," Zoe murmured.

"Oh, my God." Bree grabbed her arm. "I told you he was interested in you. What did he do? Did he jump you?"

Zoe leaned against the railing, remembering the unexpected desire that had coursed through her. The need that had shocked and overwhelmed her. "He kissed me."

"You straightened him out, didn't you? Kicked him where it hurt the most?"

"No." Zoe stepped on the paint flake, crunched it into small pieces. "I kissed him back."

"You what?" Bree sprang up and crouched in front of Zoe. "You kissed him? Gideon Tate? What the hell were you thinking?"

"That's the problem. I wasn't thinking. When he put his mouth on mine, something short-circuited in my brain. The next thing I knew, I was kissing him back and his hands were all over me." And hers were all over Gideon.

"You went to bed with him?" Bree stared at her, appalled.

"No!" But it had been close. Until he'd unhooked her bra and the cool air on her bare breasts had shocked some sense into her, she'd been oblivious to everything but the desire burning her up, the need that swept her away.

"No," she said more quietly. "It didn't go beyond a few kisses and a little…touching. I told him it wasn't going to happen again, but he just made fun of me." She wrapped her arms around herself. "He's Derrick's brother! My mind knows how stupid it would be to get involved with another man from that family. But apparently my body hasn't gotten the memo."

"You're kind of stressed out right now, Zo." Bree settled on the stair and wrapped her arm around Zoe's shoulder. "You've got the thing with Wallace, and we're cleaning out Dad's house, and now you have Gideon Tate. No wonder you're not thinking straight. Maybe all the pressure just threw your hormones out of whack. Maybe it'll be fine once everything's under control. Maybe you'll look at Gideon Tate and go, 'What was I *thinking?*'"

"Maybe." Zoe didn't think so. She'd wanted to call him back the moment he'd walked out the door last night. And how stupid did that make her? "Thanks for listening, Bree." She managed a smile. "I'll listen to you whine when you meet a guy who makes you hot and bothered."

Bree turned away. "Don't worry, Zo. That's not going to happen."

"Of course it will. I've seen how men look at you. One of these days you'll find one that makes you want to look back. When that happens, I'll save you from yourself." She tucked a strand of hair behind Bree's ear and smiled. "If you want to be saved."

Bree shook her head. "Even if I wanted to look back, I won't. I'm going to concentrate on raising Charlie."

"Why?" A sudden, horrible thought made Zoe sit down abruptly. "Bree! Did something awful happen that you haven't told us about? While you were working? Or in college? Were you assaulted?"

"Nothing like that," Bree said. She set her elbows on her knees and stared into the distance. "He was just a baby when I was doing it, but I'm terrified that Charlie will find out about the stripping. A kid shouldn't have to deal with that kind of stuff about his mother. That's why I left Milwaukee after the school found out. I knew Charlie would hear about it sooner or later."

"What does that have to do with dating?"

Bree gave her a cynical look. "Do you think I could

get involved with someone without eventually explaining about my sordid past? And if I start telling people, Charlie is bound to find out."

"He's going to discover your secret one day, Bree. Kids always do, you know." She'd seen that too many times in the troubled families that came through her shelter. "You can't keep it from him forever."

"I can until he's old enough to deal with it," her sister said fiercely. "Old enough to understand why I did it. Old enough to ignore the teasing and crude remarks."

"You're going to live like a nun until Charlie's an adult?" Zoe said, disbelieving.

"What's wrong with that? What have you been doing in the six years since Derrick died?" Bree retorted. "How many dates have *you* been on?"

"That's different."

"How is it different?" Bree demanded.

"It was my bad judgment that made me marry a man who was an abuser," Zoe said quietly. "Knowing that, why would I want to get involved with anyone else? How can I trust myself not to do it again?" She bounded down the stairs into the backyard. "Gideon is a perfect example. He's the last man I should be interested in. But who was I kissing last night? Gideon Tate."

"Not every man is a potential wife beater," Bree said.

"Agreed. But look who I married." She bent down and yanked an emerging weed from a neglected perennial bed. "I took the psychology classes in college. I know that women go back to the same type of man, over and over. Men like their father," she said bitterly.

"You're not giving yourself enough credit," Bree said, watching Zoe in the yard. "You're a smart woman. You're capable of learning. You're not going to repeat the mistake you made with Derrick."

"That's why I was hot and heavy with his brother last night, right?"

"Zo, Gideon isn't Derrick. Maybe he's not like his half brother and his father."

"You're taking his side now?" Zoe looked at her in amazement. "The woman who thought I should have kneed him in the balls?"

"I'm just saying. Don't beat yourself up because you're attracted to him. Maybe I was wrong. Give him a chance to prove who he is."

Zoe plopped onto the bottom step. "Bree, you're the one who told me to stay away from him. Why are you changing your tune?"

"Because I didn't realize you were so insecure. That you didn't trust your judgment. You've always been so sure of yourself." She nudged her sister with her foot. "You always thought you were the boss of us when we were little. The one who told me and Fiona what to do."

"I don't know why I bothered," Zoe said, trying to lighten the conversation. "You never listened to me."

"Yeah, we were really ungrateful," Bree retorted.

Okay, apparently that was still a sore spot. "How about we agree we're both pathetic and get back to work?" Zoe said brightly. "There are a lot of clothes left in Dad's room to sort through."

Bree gave her a long, thoughtful look. "Yeah. God forbid we should talk about anything that really matters."

"Hey, I'm willing to talk as much as you are," Zoe said. "You're the one who started ragging on me because I was so bossy when we were kids."

Bree stood up. "I don't want to fight with you, Zoe. So yeah, let's get back to work."

* * *

CHARLIE WAS SLOUCHED at the kitchen table, reading one of his reptile books, Bree was making the batter for popovers and Zoe was stirring a pot of stew on the stove a few hours later when the phone rang. Zoe glanced at the caller ID. "It's Fee." She picked it up. "Hey, Fee. What's up?"

She listened for a moment and her hands began to sweat. "What do you mean, pretend to be you?" Zoe's voice rose and Bree turned around to look at her. "Fiona, that's crazy talk."

"Please, Zoe, you have to do this for me." Fiona's pleading voice held an edge of desperation. "There's no way I can make it back to Spruce Lake in time for the jewelry show."

"Don't you mean there's no way you *want* to come back?" Zoe answered.

There was a momentary silence on the other end of the line. Finally Fiona said quietly, "You're right, Zo, I don't want to come back. I take my business seriously. I made a commitment to that store, and I intended to keep it. But something's come up here that I have to finish and it would be a real hassle to fly to Wisconsin just for the day." Her voice became wheedling. "If you do it, it would mean I could get back to Spruce Lake sooner."

"How could I take your place? I don't even know what you do. Or how you do it."

"It's a meet and greet at that Pieces store in town. All you have to do is smile and talk to the customers. You can do that—you do the same thing with the shelter donors and volunteers all the time."

"They'd expect me to be an expert on jewelry, Fee. I'd look like an idiot," Zoe said. "Besides, I know a lot of people in this town, and the way you and I dress isn't exactly similar." They were about as far apart as they could get. Fiona's punky, magenta-tipped hair, trendy clothes and unusual jewelry made her stand out in a crowd. Zoe just wanted to blend in.

"She can do it," Bree called. "I'll help her."

Zoe scowled at her sister. "Butt out, Bree."

"People see what they want to see," Fiona replied. "They're expecting me, so that's who they'll see. And besides, you're going to look like me." Zoe couldn't mistake the grin in her sister's voice. "I heard Bree. She'll make sure your clothes and hair and makeup are right. And your accessories."

"I'd have to dye my hair," Zoe said, grasping for a way out. "People will guess I was pretending to be you when I become Zoe again, but my hair stays Fiona."

"Not a problem," Bree interjected. "We'll use temporary dye."

Zoe sighed. She couldn't think of another excuse. "Fine. I'll take your place at Pieces and pretend to be you, Fee. But you're going to owe me, big-time. You're going to get your butt back to Spruce Lake and you're not going anywhere until we're finished with the house."

There was a pause. Then Fiona said, "Of course. I'll be back as soon as I can, and I'll stay until the end. I never intended to dump the job on you and Bree."

"I know," Zoe said. "I realize how hard this is for you, Fee. But it'll go quickly with three of us." She grabbed a pen and a piece of paper. "Now give me a crash course in your jewelry."

ZOE RESISTED brushing her palm over her spiky, pink-tipped hair. Instead, she twisted the moonstone-and-silver ring that adorned her right hand and smoothed her fingers down the long, multicolored smock she wore over black leggings. The moonstone-and-lapis pendant was heavy on her neck and the long spirals of silver dangling from her ears brushed her throat when she moved.

Judy Baer, the owner of the eclectic boutique Pieces, clasped her beringed fingers together and beamed at Zoe. "I'm so thrilled that you could make it today, Fiona," she gushed. "I'm excited that we're carrying your jewelry. You have a lot of fans in Spruce Lake."

Zoe smiled. "I'm honored that you wanted me here, Judy." Fiona's voice was a little lower and quieter than her own, and Zoe concentrated on sounding like her sister. "FeeMac Designs is excited about having an outlet in my hometown."

"And we're going to make a big deal out of it," Judy assured her. "You're just like your dear father, putting Spruce Lake on the map." The older woman fidgeted with her heavy amber necklace and sighed. "I still remember the hoopla when he won that Pulitzer for his book. There were reporters here for weeks."

John Henry McInnes had eaten up the attention and begged for more, Zoe thought grimly. "That's kind of you," Zoe forced herself to say with a smile. "But my jewelry collection isn't in the same league as a Pulitzer Prize."

"For me it is. I never read your father's book," Judy confided. "Not my cup of tea. But your jewelry!" The store owner touched a pair of silver-and-malachite earrings that glittered on the display rack. "I adored your designs the first time I saw them at a trade show. And the fact that you grew up in Spruce Lake just makes it more exciting."

Zoe glanced at the crowd of people waiting for the store to open. She'd had no idea Fiona was such a celebrity in the jewelry world. "What do you want me to do when the crowds come in, Judy?" Zoe said.

"Just welcome everyone to Pieces and tell them how happy you are that a store in your hometown is going to be carrying your jewelry. You are happy about it, aren't you?" she asked with a suddenly worried look.

"I'm thrilled," Zoe assured her. "Who wouldn't be?"

"Then, maybe, just talk to the people who want to buy something." Judy guided her behind the counter. "Help them pick out pieces that suit them. Customers will be thrilled to have a piece of jewelry personally selected for them by Fiona McInnes herself."

Oh, my God. She didn't have Fee's eye for style. How was she going to be able to tell what would look good on someone? "Do you have any tips, Judy?" she said, trying to keep the desperation out of her voice. "I don't usually get involved in the actual sale of my jewelry."

Judy winked. "You'll be fine. Just watch them. It's easy to tell what a customer likes. If it looks hideous, steer them gently toward something else."

Zoe wiped her damp palms down her smock. It was like counseling, she told herself. Let the client guide you. She could do this.

She had to.

"I'm going to open up now. Okay?"

"That's fine, Judy." Zoe pasted a smile on her face as the first customers rushed through the door.

CHAPTER TEN

"I LOVE THOSE EARRINGS on you. The shape is perfect, but did you see the other colors?" Zoe skimmed through the drawer to find the earrings in the pale green she'd seen earlier. The orange carnelians the customer was holding against her ear clashed badly with the woman's red hair.

The woman accepted them eagerly. "Oh, I like green much better," she said. "What kind of stone is this?"

Zoe struggled to remember the names of the gemstones her sister had always chattered about when they were kids. "Um, those are peridots," she said, hoping she was right.

"Thank you, Ms. McInnes," the woman said, admiring the green earrings in the mirror on the counter.

"You're more than welcome." Zoe took a deep breath and turned to the next customer with a smile. An hour had gone by, and she was beginning to relax. She could do this. It was like being a kid again. She and Fee had switched places often enough when they were younger. Then, it had been exciting to fool their teachers and friends.

Now, it was just scary. But no one had guessed that she was really Zoe. And the devil she'd kept firmly under control for the past six years was beginning to have fun.

A tall blond man and a girl pushed through the crowd—Jackson Grant and his daughter. Lindy ran to the counter, her eyes glowing. "Dad! Look at these earrings!"

Jackson ran his hand over his daughter's light brown hair. "They're something, Lin." He turned to Zoe and his eyes narrowed as he studied her. After barely more than a heartbeat, he said, "Hello, Fiona. I don't have to ask how you've been." He waved at the display of her jewelry. "Looks like you got everything you wanted."

Zoe stared at him, shocked. She had no idea that Fiona knew Jackson. Struggling to recover, she said, "Hello, Jackson." She nodded at Lindy. "Is this your daughter?"

"Yes, this is Lindy. She's a big fan. Ironic, isn't it?"

She wondered what Jackson was talking about, but she was so relieved he hadn't seen through her disguise that she pushed her curiosity to the back of her mind and smiled at the girl. "Hi, Lindy. Are you looking for something special?"

"She's looking for something appropriate for a twelve-year-old," Jackson said.

Lindy scowled. "Da-ad."

From the tone of her voice, Zoe guessed that the topic of what was appropriate had been discussed more than once in the Grant house. Hiding a smile, she said, "There are some smaller pendants over here that are nice for young women. They won't overwhelm your face, Lindy. You have beautiful eyes and you don't want to draw attention away from them."

"Really?" Lindy asked.

"Absolutely. Let's see what we can find. What colors do you like?"

"Blue. That's my favorite."

Zoe pulled a small, oval lapis pendant out of the drawer, along with the matching earrings, and held the earrings to the girl's cheek. "These really bring out the blue of your eyes," she said.

Five minutes later Lindy practically floated out the door, holding her father's hand and clutching the Pieces bag tightly. Zoe watched as Jackson bent to say something to his daughter, then kissed her on the head. A tiny barb of jealousy caught in her heart at the close, loving relationship between father and daughter.

"What about this pendant, Fiona?" a young woman asked, and Zoe turned back to the store and her job. The woman, a waitress at The Lake House, held out a silver pendant with a single oval moonstone.

Zoe forced herself back into character. Into having fun. "It's a beautiful piece, Sandy, but a little sedate. It's something my sister Zoe would wear with one of her business suits. You're more stylish than Zoe, so you could wear something more dramatic." She picked up a pendant of intricately twisted silver and moonstones. "This has a bit more flair."

"Wow! I love that." The woman's fingers skimmed over the shimmering stones. "Thanks."

Zoe heard a snort of laughter, quickly muffled, from behind the woman. She peered around her and saw Gideon standing to one side, watching her. He gave her a tiny smile and a wink, and Zoe froze.

He knew.

She had no idea how he'd figured it out, but he knew she wasn't Fiona.

Panicked, she glanced at Judy Baer, who had been ringing up sales all morning. Was Gideon going to tell the Pieces owner she'd been scammed? Was he going to tell everyone in the store that she wasn't Fiona McInnes, the designer of the expensive jewelry they were buying?

He drifted over to a different display case and she

couldn't see his face. Another customer claimed her attention and she struggled to focus on Mrs. Anderson, one of the high school teachers, while keeping an eye on Gideon. He showed no signs of talking to Judy, she realized with a small sigh of relief.

An hour later Gideon still lingered in the store. He'd bought something from Judy, but he hadn't left. Finally, when there were only casual browsers looking at her jewelry, he came up to the counter.

"Hello, Ms. McInnes," he said with a perfectly straight face, holding out his hand. "I'm Gideon Tate, a friend of your sister Zoe."

She had no choice but to shake his hand, but she drew hers away as fast as she could. It didn't matter. A little tingle of electricity raced up her arm. "Mr. Tate. Good to meet you." She tilted her head. "Are you related to the Tates here in town?"

"I am." Laughter lurked in his eyes. "I'm Wallace's son and Derrick's half brother."

Zoe raised her eyebrows. "And you're a friend of Zoe's? I find that hard to believe."

"I find it hard to believe that Zoe didn't tell you about me. She and I have gotten very close lately."

"Maybe you misunderstood her feelings."

"I don't think so," Gideon said. His voice deepened. "She was pretty vocal about how she felt."

She was in the middle of a store, impersonating her twin sister. She shouldn't be flirting with Gideon. Her breasts tightened, anyway. "Then it must have slipped her mind. She shares all her important news with me."

Gideon's hand brushed over hers as if it was an accident, and he winked. "Maybe some things are too private to be shared."

Judy hurried over. "Is this your young man, dear?"

"I'm a friend of her sister Zoe," Gideon said smoothly.

"A casual acquaintance," Zoe said, hoping her face wasn't flaming.

"How nice you came to support Zoe's sister," Judy said, clasping her hands to her chest. "Isn't that thoughtful, Fiona?"

"It is." Zoe managed a smile. "Thanks for coming by, Gideon. It was nice to meet you, but I can't hold you up any longer. You've already spent too much time here."

"There are so many intriguing things to see in Judy's store," he said. "I can't tear myself away."

"Aren't you sweet?" Judy said to Gideon. "Thank you." She gave them a happy smile as the door opened and a couple walked in. "You stay as long as you like, Gideon."

"Are you interested in jewelry, Mr. Tate?" Zoe asked. There had to be some way to get rid of him. Most men backed off fast when women started talking about fashion.

"The jewelry is beautiful," he answered. "But I'm more interested in the woman who's selling it."

"Judy will be very flattered," Zoe said.

Gideon grinned. "You remind me a lot of your sister Zoe," he said.

"I guess that's because we're identical twins."

"Must be." The couple who had just entered the store wandered over to the display of FeeMac jewelry, and Zoe turned to them thankfully.

"Hi, and welcome to Pieces. Can I show you some of my jewelry?"

"YOUR SISTER'S FRIEND looks like he's waiting for you," Judy said with a sidelong glance at Gideon an hour later. "Go ahead and leave." She squeezed Zoe's arm.

"You spent way more time here than I expected, and I really appreciate it."

Gideon was lounging near the door, and Zoe was far too aware of him standing there. Watching her. She'd tried to outwait him, but apparently that was impossible. "I enjoyed myself, Judy," she said. "We'll have to do it again soon." When Fiona herself could be here.

Grabbing the slouchy handbag that Bree had insisted she use, she stepped from behind the counter and walked out of the store. Gideon followed her onto the sidewalk.

"Can I walk you to your car, Fiona?" he asked.

"Bite me, Gideon. I know you know." She glanced at him. "How did you figure it out?"

"You didn't think I'd recognize you?"

"No. You were expecting my twin sister. People see what they expect to see." She gestured to her dress and her hair. "And I don't exactly look like myself today."

"Just a more exotic version." He brushed his hand over her spiky hair and she ducked to avoid his touch. "Zoe with pink hair. I think I like it."

"You haven't seen Fiona in years. So how do you know you can tell us apart? Why were you so sure it was me?" She and Fiona had traded places frequently when they were kids, and they'd never been caught.

His steps slowed. "I haven't kissed Fiona," he said in a low voice. "I haven't touched her."

Her heart stumbled. "What are you trying to do, Gideon?" she said, hating that her voice sounded breathless. "You know as well as I do that we're not going to get involved. That this insane…attraction, for lack of a better word, can't go anywhere."

"Because I'm a Tate and you're Zoe McInnes, who killed my brother."

She sucked in a breath. "Exactly."

"Derrick would be laughing his rear end off if he saw what was happening."

"No, he wouldn't. Derrick didn't have a sense of humor."

"Can we forget about the past for a minute?"

She stopped and turned to him. "Really? You want to forget what happened six years ago? That's not the impression I've gotten from you."

"Of course I can't forget it. But could we at least have a conversation about something else?"

"What's the point?" She started walking again. "No matter how you look at it, this is a bad idea."

"We'll see." He draped an arm across her shoulders. "Why were you impersonating your sister in that store?"

She shrugged his arm away. "Fiona had a business commitment in New York. It was easier for me to impersonate her than for her to come back to Spruce Lake."

"Easier for who?"

"Fiona, of course."

"Was it easy for you?" he asked quietly, all traces of joking gone from his voice.

She was about to brush him off with a flip remark when she made the mistake of glancing at him. The concern in his eyes was genuine.

He wasn't flirting or teasing. He cared about her answer. Some of the ice around her heart began to melt.

"I was nervous," she admitted, exhaling some of the tension. "Fee and I used to do this all the time as kids. It's fun to fool the grown-ups when you're ten years old. Fooling everyone as an adult is a lot different."

"Since you don't resemble Zoe, I'm guessing you look the part."

She brushed her hand self-consciously over her hair. "Yeah, well, she's an artist. I'll never have her flair."

"You have plenty of flair. Just a different kind."

She elbowed him in the side. "You better watch it, Gideon. If someone heard you, word might get around that you're being nice to me. Wallace would never live it down."

"I don't much care what my father thinks. Just like he doesn't care what I think."

She stumbled, shocked by his words. "You don't care about your father? Then what are you doing here?"

"I had no choice. There isn't anyone else."

"I guess that explains why no one's seen you in Spruce Lake for years."

"That's a longer story." He slowed and turned her to face him. "Have dinner with me tonight, and I'll tell you about it."

"Sorry," she said lightly, not sure if she was relieved or disappointed. "I have plans."

"A date?"

She wished! Maybe that would help her forget how she'd felt when Gideon kissed her. "Not that it's any of your business, but no. I'm building new bookcases for the living room at the shelter. We've had so many books donated that we need more shelf space."

"Building bookcases, huh? You're a woman of many talents."

"I'm not doing the actual construction—I'm dangerous with a hammer in my hand. I'm supervising."

"Need any help?"

"I can supervise just fine on my own."

"I meant with the building part. I've done some woodworking."

She slowed her steps. "You're offering to come to the shelter to do me a favor?" A thought occurred to her, and she scowled. "Is this a ruse to talk to Barb Johnson?"

"Of course not." He actually looked offended. "Communities need women's shelters. I'm a prosecutor, Zoe. I know how important they are."

"So you're willing to spend your evening building bookcases for a shelter in a town you don't even like."

"Yeah, I guess I am."

"And you know how to put together a bookcase?"

"I've built a few of them in my time."

She studied him for a moment, but couldn't see any hint of an underlying agenda. "All right," she finally said. "We can use all the help we can get. But if you try to talk to Barb, I'll throw you out in a heartbeat."

"Speaking of Barb," he said in a low voice, nodding at the parking lot. "That's Dave Johnson coming toward us."

CHAPTER ELEVEN

GIDEON FELT ZOE tense beside him. He took her elbow to steady her, surprised when she didn't shake him off.

"Hey, Gideon," Dave called, waving. "Hold on a sec."

"Let me go," she said. "Right now."

He dropped his hand, but Dave had already seen him holding on to Zoe and his face hardened.

"You're Zoe McInnes, aren't you?" he said.

"I'm her sister Fiona," Zoe answered. She'd changed her voice again to the one she'd used in the store. Lower-pitched than her own. And slower. Gideon watched her, amused and intrigued.

"Do you know Dave Johnson, Fiona?" Gideon asked.

Zoe gave Dave a cool smile and didn't offer to shake hands. "I do now."

"Hi." Dave shifted his feet. "I, ah, thought you were your sister," he finally said.

"I get that a lot," Zoe answered. Gideon swallowed a grin.

Dave's gaze swept over her. "Up close, you don't look like Zoe at all," he said.

"Really?" she answered. "Zoe and I are identical."

"Well, you look a lot different. More adventurous." He stepped closer. "Wilder. How long are you in town?"

"Not long enough to be wild," Zoe said lightly. "Nice meeting you, Dave. Goodbye, Gideon."

Gideon watched until she got into her car, then turned on Dave. Jealousy, completely unjustified, washed through him. Along with irritation. "I don't believe it. You were putting the moves on her."

Dave shrugged. "She's hot. Not like her ball-breaker sister."

"Are you out of your mind?" Gideon said sharply. "You're married. Your wife is in Zoe's shelter. Do you think it's going to help your cause when Zoe finds out you were flirting with her sister?"

Dave waved his hand dismissively. "What's wrong with flirting with a beautiful woman? You take things too seriously, man."

"I'm your attorney, *man*," Gideon answered. "It's my job to take things seriously. Especially when my client is making an ass of himself."

"That's a little harsh, Gid."

Gideon stared at him without speaking. Apparently he didn't know his brother's friend as well as he thought. Dave's smile faded. "Okay, you're right. I'm being a jerk." He raked his hand through his hair. "My only excuse is that I'm worried about Barb."

"You have a damned odd way of showing it."

"I do stupid things when I'm nervous," Dave said.

Gideon sighed, "Forget it. Were you looking for me?"

"No, but I was going to call you later. I may have a witness who saw Barb fall off that ladder."

"Really?"

"Yeah. Mrs. Kowalczyk. She lives behind us."

"That's great. How did you find her?" Gideon asked, his annoyance with Dave fading.

"I talked to all my neighbors, asked them if they remembered seeing Barb on a ladder cleaning out the gutters. Mrs. Kowalczyk said she did."

"Good work." Gideon clapped him on the back. "I'll go talk to her."

"I guess you have to do that, don't you?" Dave said.

"Of course I have to talk to her. Is there some reason I shouldn't?" Gideon looked more carefully at Dave.

"She's old, so you have to ease into things with her."

"I know how to handle witnesses, Dave. Even elderly ones."

"Yeah, that's why I wanted you to help me," Dave said. "You're the best, Gideon. You'll get this mess with Barb straightened out."

Zoe's car pulled out of the parking lot and disappeared around a corner. "I'll do my best, but you need to watch yourself," he retorted. "Pissing Zoe off isn't going to help your case."

"Chill, man. I was making conversation." Dave frowned. "When did you turn into such a prude?"

"The day I agreed to defend you," Gideon said. "*Making conversation* with one of Zoe's sisters is flat-out stupid."

"Yeah, yeah. I got it. I'll live like a monk."

"Good. I'll go visit your Mrs. Kowalczyk. Do you have her address?" He scribbled it on a notepad, then waved goodbye to Dave.

"How did it go?" Bree looked up from the kitchen sink as Zoe walked in the back door.

"Good. Judy Baer sold lots of FeeMac jewelry."

Bree set the dish she'd been washing in the dish drainer and dried her hands. "Fee just called. She thought you'd be back by now. We were both a little worried."

"Really? How come?"

"The event was supposed to last two hours, and you've been gone four. Anything could have happened."

"In big, bad downtown Spruce Lake?"

"Something might have gone wrong. You bet we were worried." Bree plopped down on a kitchen chair. "Did anyone guess you weren't Fiona?"

Zoe tossed the purse that was so much more Fiona's style than hers onto another chair. "One person."

"Oh, my God. Who?"

Before answering, Zoe got herself a glass of water and drank deeply. The stress of deceiving everyone, with Gideon as her audience, had drained her. Setting the empty glass on the counter, she avoided looking at her sister. "Gideon."

"Gideon Tate was there?"

"He spent the whole morning in the store." Zoe yanked open the refrigerator and stared inside. Hamburger, lettuce and jelly weren't going to make much of a lunch. "Watching me."

"Did he tell Judy?"

"He never said a word and he played along like I was Fiona. But he knew." He'd known from the instant he stepped into the store and saw her. As she relived the moment their eyes met, something fluttered in her chest.

"Why didn't he bust you?" Bree asked. She jumped up from her chair. "What does he want?"

Zoe shut the refrigerator. "I don't know," she said. "But he's helping build bookcases at the shelter tonight."

"You're letting him work at the shelter?" Bree stared at her, appalled.

"Yeah. What's wrong with that?" The excitement

that had been fizzing in Zoe's veins began to go flat. "He said he's done some woodworking."

"You don't see a problem with letting a Tate into Safe Harbor?"

"You said yourself he's not his brother. Or his father. He's willing to do it, and we need all the volunteers we can get."

Bree studied her. "I was right. There is something going on between you two. Be careful, Zo."

"I'm always careful." Especially where men were concerned. "Careful's my middle name."

"I think your middle name is *totally whacked*."

"For God's sake, Bree. We'll be in the shelter. With at least ten other people around. What do you think is going to happen?"

"God only knows. But you see a man working with his hands, it does something to you."

"It makes me grateful that he knows how to put up a bookcase," Zoe retorted. "That's all."

"You've been acting different since Gideon showed up," Bree said. "Not like yourself."

"What's myself?"

"You're the careful one, Zo. You don't even go out on dates. Now you're kissing this guy one night and inviting him to your shelter the next?"

"The kiss was a mistake. And the shelter is business."

Bree looked at Zoe's hair and clothes. "Did you absorb some of Fee's wildness from her outfit?"

Zoe touched her hair. She'd always been the sensible McInnes sister, the one who did what she was supposed to do. "Maybe I'd like being wild," she said lightly.

"Okay, now I'm really worried."

"Can't you tell when I'm yanking your chain?"

"Not funny, Zo."

"Jackson Grant and his daughter, Lindy, came into the store and bought some of Fee's jewelry," Zoe said, trying to change the subject. "He seemed to know Fiona pretty well. Any idea what that's about?"

"Not a clue," Bree answered.

"Anyway, Jackson was very sweet with Lindy." She recalled the little twinge of jealousy she'd felt.

"They're a nice family."

"Good daddy material," Zoe said lightly.

"For someone else." Bree stood up. "Your hormones are really worked up, aren't they? I told you I'm not interested. Not in him or anyone else." Bree's voice rose, a sure sign of her temper building. But instead of snapping, she took a deep breath. "Butt out, Zo. Please."

"Sorry," Zoe said. "I really am." What was with her hormones? "Apparently I have men on the brain."

"I think that's 'man,' as in one in particular." Bree put her hands on Zoe's shoulders. "Take care, okay? I don't want to see you hurt again."

Zoe hugged her. "There's nothing to worry about. He's just like any other volunteer at the shelter."

"I'M STILL SURPRISED you agreed to let me come tonight," Gideon said as he backed out of Zoe's driveway.

"We can always use an extra pair of hands," she said with a shrug. "Especially someone who knows how to put bookcases together. I'm willing to overlook your downside."

"And that would be?" he asked, shifting gears, biting his lip to hide a smile. He enjoyed Zoe's bluntness. Some people might find it disconcerting, but he liked knowing what she was thinking.

If her words hadn't let him know, the way she was pressed against her side of the car would have tipped him off. She clearly didn't want any accidental touches while he shifted gears.

"Who you are, of course." She glanced at him as if surprised he'd had to ask. "Tates and Safe Harbor don't exactly go together. Having you help out at the shelter is like something out of *The Twilight Zone*."

"I've never been called a supernatural phenomenon before," he said.

"I wouldn't say supernatural. Odd, maybe. Definitely unexplainable."

He wasn't sure himself why he'd volunteered. Curiosity, he supposed. Seeing Zoe in the shelter she'd created and ran might give him new insight into her. Insight he needed to help Dave, he told himself.

Boredom probably played a role, too. He was going crazy, sitting around Spruce Lake with nothing to do but visit his father in the hospital.

It wasn't because he wanted to spend more time with Zoe herself.

"Are we building these things from scratch?" he asked.

"God, no. A furniture store in Sturgeon Falls donated four bookcases," Zoe said. "But they have to be put together. We need tools and people who know how to use them, so I thought we'd make a party out of it. Some of our donors and volunteers, plus a couple of former residents of the shelter, will be there."

Following Zoe's directions, he pulled up in front of a large, rambling house that was a hodgepodge of several different styles. "This is it?"

"It's not much to look at," she said defensively. "The last owner liked to add on. But it has lots of room."

"I wasn't criticizing," he assured her. "It's fascinating."

"It's a mess, is what it is. But it's my mess." She pulled her toolbox out of the backseat.

Their hands brushed as he took it from her. Ignoring the zip of electricity that ran up his arm, he pretended to study the hideous architecture of the house. It kept him from reaching out to touch her again.

An explosion of noise greeted him as they walked in the front door. Women and children and a couple of men filled the large living room to their right. The furniture looked like hand-me-downs, but it was all sturdy and clean. The walls were decorated with paintings, some prints of famous impressionists, others more modern.

"Hey, everyone," Zoe said. "This is Gideon. He's going to help out tonight. He's built bookcases before."

"Hi, Gideon," people called out, welcoming him with smiles and waves. He recognized Zoe's attorney and one of the Spruce Lake cops in the crowd. The attorney raised her eyebrows. Zoe shrugged.

"You can leave your jacket in my office," Zoe said in a low voice, opening the door across the hall.

Her office was as messy as the living room was orderly. Papers and books covered the surface of her desk and were piled onto two of the chairs, and children's drawings similar to the ones at her home were pinned up everywhere. A corkboard with pictures of women and children hung behind her desk.

She slung her coat on a rack behind the door. Her red, V-neck sweater revealed a hint of shadowed cleavage when she reached out to take his jacket.

She froze when she saw the direction of his gaze, then quickly straightened. Hanging his jacket on a hook, she said brightly, "Let's get started."

Zoe was good at organizing, he admitted. She put four people in charge, one for each bookcase, then assigned helpers to each group. He laid out the screws and pegs on the floor, flattered she'd asked him to head up one of the teams.

As he read the instructions for assembling the bookcase, he watched Zoe circulate. She hugged the children, saying something personal to each of them, and laughed and joked with the volunteers. She spoke encouragingly to the shelter residents, giving each a pat on the shoulder or a touch on the arm. It wasn't hard to spot them—they all had a pinched look to their faces, as if it had been too long since they'd smiled.

Barb Johnson was working with one of the other groups. The farthest one from him, he noticed with a smile. She looked as if the weight of the world lay heavy on her shoulders. Was Dave really telling the truth? He made a mental note to visit Mrs. Kowalczyk as soon as possible.

Zoe was amazing. If she'd been anyone else besides his former sister-in-law, he'd have been interested in her. Hell, he was already attracted. Enough that guilt stabbed into him whenever he looked at her.

He focused on the pieces of pine on the floor in front of him and swung his hammer at a nail. Too hard. The hammer slipped and dented the soft wood.

By the time they were done, even the residents were relaxed and smiling. The whole crowd stood back and admired the finished bookcases, then moved them into place against the walls. Zoe stepped into the middle of the crowd and said, "Thank you, everyone, for all your hard work. Next week we'll start filling the shelves with the books we've received."

She hugged a young girl who stood next to her. "I think there are some more *Harry Potter*s in those boxes, Ashley. Are you finished with the first one yet?"

"Yes!" the girl said, jumping up and down. "I can't wait to read number two."

"I'll help you look for it tonight, if you like."

A rail-thin woman put her arm around Ashley's shoulders. "I'll find it for her, Zoe. You must have better ways to spend your Saturday night." She glanced at Gideon with a shy smile.

Zoe avoided Gideon's eyes. "Thanks, Sue. The boxes are in the garage."

The residents looked at the bookcases, clearly proud of what they'd accomplished, and Gideon didn't want the evening to end. "I'm hungry after all that work," he said loudly. "I bet everyone else is, too. How about we get some pizza to celebrate a job well done?"

CHAPTER TWELVE

"THANKS AGAIN for coming to the shelter tonight," Zoe said as she opened her front door. "You were a big help."

"Is that your standard volunteer speech?" he asked as he followed her into the house. "If so, it could use a little more zip. Maybe you could say you'd have been lost without me. Or no one has ever done a better job."

Was he *teasing* her? "You do swing a pretty mean hammer," she said, closing the door behind him. "And what you can do with a screwdriver is magic." Not to mention how kind and careful he'd been to all the women. And how he'd had the children giggling.

"I'm good with a lot of tools," he said with a straight face.

She couldn't stop herself from laughing. "Oh, God. I haven't heard that line since high school."

"Hey, I stick with what works," he said.

She hadn't intended to invite him in. She'd planned on thanking him and saying good-night. But her preconceived ideas about Gideon had been turned on their ear this evening. Now she was even more curious about him.

"Would you like a beer? Or some wine?"

"A beer sounds good."

When she returned from the kitchen with his Leinie and a glass of wine for herself, he was studying the pictures on the wall. "Did the girl who wanted to read the *Harry Potter* book draw this?" he asked, pointing at a picture of a stick figure with glasses holding a wand.

"Yep, that's Ashley's." Remembering the girl's joy in the story, Zoe smiled. "I don't think she'd ever read a book for pleasure before the first *Harry Potter.*"

"You impressed me tonight," he said, taking a drink of his beer and holding her gaze. "In a lot of ways."

"You flatterer, you," she said, uncomfortable with the intensity in his eyes.

"You connect with those women. They all adore you."

"They're not afraid for the first time in a long time. That's all it is."

"Hmm." He set the beer on her coffee table and lowered himself to the couch. "And what was up with your attorney and the cop? Why did you put them in the same group? They bickered the whole time."

"Helen and Jamie," she said, sitting in the chair next to him, grateful he'd changed the subject. "They're interested in each other, but neither of them will make the first move. I was just throwing a few logs on the fire."

"You're a romantic," Gideon said, sipping his beer. "I never would have guessed."

"It's easy to be a romantic with other people's lives," she said lightly.

"But not your own."

"I'm a realist." She looked at his arm, stretched across the back of the couch, and remembered the ropy muscle beneath his skin from the other night. *I need to be realistic about Gideon.* "I'd guess you are, too."

"I think I'm surprising myself," he said, shifting to face her. He stretched his legs out on either side of hers, brushing against them. Her legs were caught between his for a moment. Then he released her. She sucked in her breath, but he didn't seem to notice.

How is he surprising himself? Best not to go there. "Tell me about when you were a kid in Spruce Lake," she said, scrambling to steady herself.

"Need to get the defenses up, Zoe?"

"What do you mean?" It took every bit of her composure to look at him steadily.

He sat up and shifted his legs so she was trapped once again. "The best way to deflect any unwanted attention is to ask a tough question."

"Unwanted attention? You think I'm worried that I'll swoon if you touch me? That I'll turn into helpless putty in your hands?"

"I saw a part of you tonight I'd never seen before. A part of you I suspect you keep pretty well hidden, except when you're at that shelter," he said, reaching toward her and smoothing a finger over the back of her hand. Her breath hitched. "Who knows what that might lead to?"

She tried to laugh, but it sounded more like a moan.

His finger stopped moving. After a long moment he picked up her hand. "Let's find out," he said as he pressed a kiss against her wrist. His voice vibrated against her skin, making other parts of her throb.

"I'm not swooning," she said, trying to keep her voice from trembling.

He smiled. "I'll try harder." He touched his tongue to her wrist, then gently sucked. Nerves jumped in her belly, and she bit her lip to keep from gasping.

He raised his head, his mouth still on her wrist. "Anything?"

"N-no," she managed. She wanted to leap onto the couch and fasten her mouth to his.

"I guess you're right," he said, setting her hand on her thigh and covering it with his. "You're immune to me. I need to work on my technique."

She bit off a plea for him to kiss her wrist again and drew her hand away. "Yes," she said. "It had absolutely no effect."

"Right. So what do you want to know about my childhood?"

"Your childhood?" she asked. All she could think about was the way her body wanted him.

"You had a question," he reminded her gently. She thought she saw a twinkle in his eye.

"Yes. I did." She licked her lips. "Spruce Lake. When you were a kid."

"My mother and I lived here until I was twelve," he said. "Then we moved to Milwaukee. I didn't see my father after that."

"Why not?"

His smile disappeared. "When my mother announced we were leaving town, Dad pitched a fit. He didn't want my mother taking me away, even though I only saw him two weekends a month. I liked having a brother, but I didn't know Derrick's mom very well. She was quiet and never said much. To anyone in the family."

"So you went with your mother." The flush of desire was fading and Zoe was regaining her composure.

"Yes. My father wanted me to stay with him. He got angry when I said I was going with Mom, and he said if I left, I couldn't ever come back and see him or Derrick."

The scenes with her own father flashed into Zoe's mind, and she took his hand. "He made you choose between him and your mother?"

"I chose my mother, of course. I didn't want to leave Derrick behind, but I hardly knew my dad. And I was never comfortable with him, or in his house," he said.

"Why didn't you come to the wedding? I sent you an invitation." She'd hoped to please Derrick by reconnecting him with his brother.

"I intended to come. Then I was uninvited."

"Derrick told you not to come?"

"Dad did."

"And you listened to him? You and Derrick were both adults. Why didn't you tell Wallace to butt out?"

"Derrick didn't want anything to do with me. Wallace probably convinced him I was the devil."

"Derrick always did whatever Wallace told him to do."

"Even when you were married to him?"

She rubbed her suddenly sweaty hands on her jeans. "Even then. Wallace must have hated you for getting away."

"He's not happy I'm back, either. That I have power over him."

"He should be grateful," she said fiercely. "That you're willing to be here."

"I don't expect anything from him, including gratitude. I'm doing my duty, nothing more."

"But you stepped up to the plate. That's admirable."

He got to his feet and gestured toward her fireplace. "Enough about Wallace. Would you like me to build a fire?"

"It's gas. All you have to do is turn it on. I'm not good at starting real fires. They always smoke too much and burn too little."

"Make it hot enough, there's no smoke." He was looking at her, not at the grate.

Oh, God. She was in so much trouble. Her face flushed, her body on fire, she watched him check the flue and turn on the gas. Then he took her hand and pulled her out of the chair and onto the couch next to him.

"Satisfied with my life story?" he murmured.

No. She wanted to know more about him. "When did you decide to become a lawyer?"

"Truth? At your trial. You shot my brother and got away with it, and that was hard to stomach. I went to law school and joined the DA's office in Milwaukee."

She laughed. She couldn't help it. "So it's my fault you're a lawyer? And now we're on opposite sides in Barb Johnson's case. Apparently God has a sense of humor."

"Sure looks that way. How else would I have ended up sitting in your living room, having a drink with you?"

"Who'd have guessed?" she agreed.

His hand rested on her shoulder and his fingers dangled close to the side of her breast. If she inhaled deeply, they'd touch her. "You're the last woman I ever thought I'd be with. I can't want you."

"I know," she said. Her voice sounded hoarse. "I can't want you, either."

"I *don't* want you, Zoe." His fingers brushed her breast once. Accidentally, she was almost sure.

"I don't want you, either. Or anything to do with anyone named Tate." She moved slightly, just enough for his fingers to graze her again.

"So what's going on here?"

"We're having a drink and watching the fire. That's all." But her body throbbed and desire roared through her veins. How could she want him? What was wrong with her?

"Is it?" He leaned closer until he was almost touching her ear. Close enough that if she turned her head, her mouth would be against his. "Maybe we should test that hypothesis."

She was in so far over her head she wasn't sure she'd ever surface for air. Struggling for control, she said, "I always did like the scientific method."

"Good to know." Their lips were separated by less than an inch. He cupped her face in his hands and brushed his mouth over hers.

It was barely a kiss, but it made her tremble. She felt him tense, then he kissed her again.

This time wasn't gentle. This was heat and fire and need burning through her, marking her. Someone groaned, and she was afraid it was her. She wrapped her arms around him, desperate for the press of his chest against her breasts, the hardness of his muscles against her softness.

The kiss went on and on, tongues tangling, hands roaming restlessly over each other. He eased her onto her back and she pulled him close. She slid her hands beneath his sweater and he froze. While she explored his chest, the muscles and coarse hair she'd been longing to feel since the night she'd interrupted his boxing, he held himself above her. Watching her.

"I wanted to touch you that night," she whispered. "When you'd been boxing. I thought I'd lost my mind."

She caressed the hard nubs of his nipples. He pulled her roughly into his arms and took the kiss deeper, into a dark, hot place where nothing existed but his mouth, his tongue, his hands. Covering her breasts, weighing them in his palms.

He shoved her sweater up, pausing to stare at her bra. "I like black lace," he muttered, bending to kiss the tip of one breast through the material. "I like it better with you in it."

His mouth barely made contact with her nipple, but she arched against him with a shocked cry. He fumbled for the clasp and undid it, letting the bra fall open.

"Beautiful," he whispered as he stroked her, his fingers smoothing over her skin and between her breasts. He circled close to her nipple, then away. Never touching.

"Touch me, Gideon," she said, barely recognizing her voice. "Please." She ached for him. Wrapping one leg around his, she pulled him down to her. He settled between her legs, his erection pressing into her.

He took her breast in his mouth, and she sobbed his name. Her hands shook as she pulled his sweater over his head, then fumbled with his buckle. She couldn't get any further because he was pressed into the cradle of her legs, rubbing against her, suckling her breast, driving her higher and higher.

"Come for me, Zoe," he whispered as he rocked. "I want to watch you."

His words pushed her over the edge and she shattered, clinging to him as the pleasure went on and on. Finally he cradled her face in his palms. "I guess you do want me, Zoe."

Reality returned as her heart slowed, and she was mortified. "Why did you do that, Gideon?" she said. "I was… I wanted…not alone."

He trailed his fingers down her cheek. "Do you know how sexy it is, how hard it makes me, to know I made you come like that?" He replaced his hand with his cheek, and his five-o'clock shadow rasped against her skin. "We have all night. And we're going to need it."

He peeled her sweater off her arms, followed by her bra. They were both naked from the waist up, fully clothed otherwise. He grinned at her. "I like the look. But I'd like it better if you lost the pants."

He slid off her and unbuttoned his own pants, letting them fall. His legs were muscled, his abdomen hard and flat. His erection strained at his silk boxers.

Derrick had worn boxers like that.

The thought was a splash of ice water in her face. What was she doing? How did she get from keeping her distance, from handling Gideon, to making love with him?

She reddened as she struggled to sit up. He'd been the one doing the handling.

"What's wrong?" he asked, sitting down next to her and wrapping his arm around her. "Are you getting cold feet? Having second thoughts?"

"That would make me a real jerk," she said. She wanted to have sex with him, wanted to take off the rest of her clothes and lead him to her bed.

"You're allowed to change your mind."

She trembled, and it wasn't from passion. Gideon eased away from her. "It's okay, Zoe. I understand."

"Don't be such a nice guy. Get mad. Yell at me or something." Make her feel less guilty.

He looked at her bare chest, then handed her her sweater. She pulled it on without bothering with her bra. The black lace lay on the floor. Gideon followed her gaze, then stood up and pulled on his own clothes.

"Do you want me to leave?"

She didn't want him to go. She wanted him to stay. But that wouldn't be fair. "I guess it would be best." She got to her feet and touched his cheek. "I'm sorry, Gideon."

"Yeah, me, too." He ran his hand down her chest,

touched one still-hard nipple. "But I can wait for you to catch up."

"It's been a long time for me," she said. "There hasn't been anyone since…" Since Derrick. No one else knew that. She hated to make herself vulnerable, to let him see her insecurities, but she owed him that, at least, for being so generous.

"No?" His eyes darkened, but he said, "Then we'll take it slow." He drew her into his arms, kissed her with both passion and gentleness, and the embers of desire flamed to life again. She felt his response as she kissed him back, then he eased away from her. "Okay, Zoe?"

"Okay. But I do want you, Gideon," she whispered.

He closed his eyes with a groan. "I need to leave, Zoe. *Now.* Or I'll break my promise."

A chink opened in the wall around her heart, and she wasn't sure she could close it again. Wasn't sure she wanted to. Before she could process the fear and anticipation flowing through her, her cell phone rang with the shelter's tone. She found her purse, fumbled in it.

"Hello?"

"We need you over here, Zoe," her housemother Sharon said. "ASAP."

"Okay. I'll be right there." Now there was no question Gideon had to leave. She wasn't sure if she was relieved or disappointed. "I have to go to the shelter."

"Right now?"

"The police probably brought a woman to us. They always need to talk to someone right away."

"Okay. I'll drive you over."

"You don't have to do that, Gideon." A sweet lightness moved through her. "I've screwed up your evening enough already."

"Yeah, you have. But I'm a glutton for punishment. Get your stuff together and let's go."

Tenderness tugged at her heart. "I do this all the time. I could probably drive over there blindfolded."

"Not feeling the way you do now." He smoothed his hand down her face, took her hand.

She brushed her mouth over his. "I need to drive myself so I have a way to get home."

"Then I'll follow you to make sure you get there safely."

She was the one who took care of other people. No one had ever taken care of her. "I'd like that, Gideon."

CHAPTER THIRTEEN

"I'M GLAD YOU'RE BACK, Fee," Zoe said as she sat at the kitchen table in their father's house, her hands wrapped around a mug of tea. Bree was drinking another of her endless cups of coffee, and Fiona wasn't drinking anything. She drummed her fingers on the table.

Fiona shrugged. "I wish I could say I was, too, but I'm not going to lie."

"Dad's not here anymore," Bree said gently. "He can't hurt us."

"I know." Fiona jumped up and paced the small kitchen. "But this place has too many memories. Too much *stuff*." She stopped and faced her sisters. "I thought I'd put all this behind me. I guess I haven't."

"We'll get the house cleaned out and then we can all go back home," Zoe said. But the idea depressed her. She wanted her sisters in her life, not leading separate existences on the fringes of hers.

"Good," Fiona said. "I know you two have been busy while I was gone. I'll try to make up for it."

Bree smiled around her mug of coffee. "Zo's certainly been busy."

"I know she has," Fiona said, sitting down again. "Thank you so much for making the appearance at the store. It was a huge help."

Zoe smiled. "I was a little nervous at first, but everyone accepted that I was you." Well, almost everyone. "And I sold a butt-load of your jewelry."

"I wasn't talking about her appearance at Pieces," Bree said. She set the mug down and raised her eyebrows at Zoe. "But that's a good place to start. Not everyone thought you were Fiona, did they, Zo?"

Zoe cleared her throat. "Gideon knew I wasn't you."

"Oh, no. Did he tell Judy? Did he make a scene?"

While Zoe tried to figure out how to brush over the subject of Gideon, Bree jumped in. "He played along. And Zoe took him to the shelter that night to build bookcases."

Fiona stared at her. "You took him to Safe Harbor?"

"He was volunteering, for heaven's sake. Lots of people volunteer. Why is this such a big deal?"

"What happened after the bookcases were finished?" Bree asked. "Did he drop you off at home and disappear? Did he come inside? We want details, Zo."

"There are no details." Zoe felt her face flaming and knew she was giving herself away.

"I don't know about Fiona," Bree said, "but it's been so long since I had a love life that I've pretty much forgotten how it works. You're the only one getting any action, Zoe. So spill."

Zoe sighed. "He bought pizza for everyone at the shelter, then we went back to my house and had a drink."

Fiona propped her chin on her hand. "Then what?"

"Then I got a call from the shelter and had to go back there. Jesse Halvorsen was making threatening calls to his wife's cell phone, and she was hysterical. I spent the rest of the night at Safe Harbor."

Bree raised one eyebrow. "We want to know what happened between the drinks and the shelter," she said.

"Stuff that shouldn't have happened," Zoe muttered.

"Oh, my God," Bree said, almost spilling her coffee.

"Zoe!" Fiona said. "This guy is Derrick's brother!"

"Gideon isn't Derrick. I'm not afraid of him." She was afraid of what she was beginning to feel for him.

"I don't mean physically injure you," Fiona said impatiently. "I know you're too smart to repeat that mistake. There are a lot of other ways he can hurt you."

Zoe studied her twin. "You don't let many people in, do you, Fee. No one gets close enough to hurt you."

"Why would I want to get hurt?" Fiona asked.

"If no one can hurt you, no one can make you happy, either."

"I make myself happy," she retorted.

Fiona had learned that lesson a long time ago, Zoe thought sadly. From their father. "I'm just saying, Fee. Sometimes you need to take a chance."

"Like you are with Gideon Tate?" Bree asked.

"Maybe." She took a drink of her lukewarm tea. "Look, whatever is going on between us isn't any big deal. Gideon is in town until his father gets better, then he's going back to Milwaukee. My life is here in Spruce Lake." She shrugged, but she had to work to appear casual. "Maybe I'll have a little fling."

"A fling?" Bree looked at her, incredulous. "Zoe McInnes have a fling? The next time that happens will be the first. Have you even dated anyone since Derrick died?"

"Of course."

Bree snorted. "By dating, I don't mean having dinner with a guy once a year. I mean getting involved. Getting horizontal with someone."

"You're criticizing my dating behavior? Because you both have such perfect lives?" She turned on Bree. "You don't intend to date ever again because you can't get past what you did as a kid. And Fee is so distant with everyone that she can't even bear to spend a couple of weeks with her sisters. So don't criticize me for thinking about having fun with a man."

"This isn't about us," Bree shot back. "We're talking about you right now."

"We'd be thrilled if you were seeing a guy," Fiona said. "But this is the brother of the man who beat you."

"Don't you think I know that?" Zoe said. "I can't figure it out myself." She slumped back in her chair. "I don't know what I feel about Gideon. It's complicated. Confusing." *Time to go on the offensive again.* "Why don't we talk about your lives for a change? Bree, have you gone over to the high school yet to ask about substitute teaching?"

"As a matter of fact, I have," she said, her voice smug. "I'm on the list and they told me I should be getting some calls right away."

"What about Barb Johnson's job?"

Bree fiddled with her mug. "They already filled it."

"See, you should have gone over there sooner. You—"

"I know, Zo," Bree interrupted sharply. "I screwed up. You don't have to point it out to me."

Zoe took a deep breath. As a sub, Bree wouldn't have health insurance, and she needed it. Charlie's heart condition had been surgically corrected several years earlier and he was fine, but he had to be tested every year. And that cost a lot of money. "Sorry," she said. "I worry about you."

"I know, but I've been taking care of myself and Charlie for a long time," Bree answered.

The back door slammed open and Charlie ambled in. "Hi, Mom." He glanced at Fiona and Zoe. "Hi, Aunts."

"How was school today?" Bree asked him.

"It was weird," Charlie said, taking an apple from the refrigerator, biting into it and moving to lean against his mother.

"Yeah? How so?" Bree wrapped an arm round him.

"The cops were there," he said, his eyes cautious. "They brought dogs with them. To sniff at all the lockers."

"They brought drug-sniffing dogs into middle school?" Zoe asked, shocked.

Charlie nodded. "They made me open my locker."

"What?" Bree didn't raise her voice, but her hand tightened on Charlie's shoulder.

"They looked at all my stuff and wanted to know about my inhaler. I told them about my heart thing," he said.

"Did you tell them the nurse at the school has the permission slip for the inhaler?" Bree's voice started to rise, and Zoe put her hand on her sister's arm and gave her a warning squeeze. Charlie didn't look as if he was bothered by the search. There was no reason to upset him now.

"Ms. Wilson told them," he said, tossing the apple core into the compost bucket and heading back to the fridge. "There was this one old cop, and she told him they had no business scaring the kids like that. I don't think the cop liked it."

"Probably not," Bree said, glancing at Zoe out of the corner of her eye. "Good thing we got that permission slip in to the nurse," she said more quietly.

"All the kids thought it was cool that the cops searched my locker," Charlie went on. "Nobody was scared." He rummaged in the refrigerator and came out with a carton of yogurt. "They asked me if I was in a gang in Milwaukee."

"A *gang?*"

"I told them there weren't any gangs where we lived."

"That was a good answer, Charlie," Bree managed to say. "You want to play some video games before you tackle your homework?"

"Nah. I have to clean the snakes' cages today." He grabbed another apple and went upstairs.

Bree and Fiona and Zoe looked at one another. "I'm going to nail Ray Dobbs's hide to the wall," Bree said.

"I'll help you," Zoe said. "Thank goodness Charlie's a smart kid and kept his head."

"Take it easy, you two," Fiona said. "It didn't upset Charlie. It got him attention from the other kids for something other than being the smart kid. If you make a stink, they might look at him differently."

Bree sighed and wiped a hand over her face. "Damn it, Fee. You're right. But I still want to pound on Dobbs."

Fiona shook her head. "Now do you understand why I don't want to be here? In a place where the chief of police can pick on a kid because he's got a grudge against the child's aunt?" She scowled at Zoe. "You still going to tell me that things have changed here?"

GIDEON PULLED UP to the curb of a small, white Cape Cod house. The painted clapboard was peeling and the enclosed front porch seemed to list to one side. The curtains at the front of the house were drawn.

He was counting on Mrs. Kowalczyk to be a credible witness. There wasn't anyone else.

He rang the doorbell and heard the sound of shuffling from inside. After a long time, the door opened and a white-haired woman stood there, holding on to a walker. "Mrs. Kowalczyk? I'm Gideon Tate, Dave Johnson's lawyer. He said he told you I'd be coming by."

"Dave Johnson?" The woman looked puzzled.

"Your neighbor. He lives behind you."

Her face cleared. "That's right. The nice young man who came by the other day. He brought my garbage cans in from the street and collected my mail for me."

"Dave's a thoughtful guy," Gideon said. "May I come in and talk to you?"

"Of course not," she said indignantly. "I don't know you. My daughter would be mad if I let you in the house."

"Is your daughter here? Can I talk to her?"

"Oh, no, my daughter doesn't live here. She lives on the other side of town. But she comes by to check on me almost every day."

"I'll stay on the porch, then," he said. "May I ask you some questions?"

"Questions? About what?"

"About Dave and his wife."

She looked bewildered. "That young man has a wife?"

Gideon was starting to get a bad feeling about Mrs. Kowalczyk's testimony. "Dave told me you saw his wife fall off a ladder in their backyard. Do you remember that?"

"I didn't see any ladder." She frowned. "Where did you say he lived?"

Gideon smiled at the elderly woman and cursed Dave in his mind. "Thank you, Mrs. Kowalczyk. You've been very helpful. I appreciate you talking to me."

"You're welcome, dear."

"Lock this door behind me, all right?" Gideon said.

"I always lock my doors," she assured him.

"Good." He waited until he heard the lock engage,

then he hurried to his car. Pulling his cell phone out of his pocket, he punched in Dave's number.

"What the hell are you trying to do?" he asked as soon as Dave answered.

"Gideon? What are you talking about?"

"I've just been to see Mrs. Kowalczyk," he answered. "How did you get her to say she saw Barb on a ladder?"

There was silence on the other end. "I, ah, just asked her some questions," he finally said.

"The only thing she remembers is that you're a nice young man who brought in her garbage cans and her mail. She doesn't even know who Barb is."

"She seemed to know what she was talking about," Dave said, but he sounded defensive.

"We need to get together, Dave," Gideon said. "Soon." Was Zoe right? Had Dave really hit his wife?

And if he had, what did that say about Gideon's instincts?

He couldn't count on them anymore, he admitted. His instincts had been screwed up since the moment he walked into the Spruce Lake jail and saw Zoe in a cell.

"You think I hit her?" Dave's voice rose. "I swear to you, Gideon, I've never laid a finger on Barb."

"We'll talk about this later," he said. Right now he was too angry at Dave's attempted deception to be objective. "I'll call you."

THE MUSCLES IN Zoe's legs burned, and her lungs ached from the cooling air. She'd been running for a long time, but she wasn't ready to slow down. Even though the sun had set and the sky was darkening into twilight, she'd keep running until she was exhausted enough to sleep.

Why did she and her sisters always end up fighting?

She wanted to put aside the bitterness, the wariness, the defensiveness. But years spent with their father's twisted manipulations didn't fade in a few days.

She hadn't been back to the old house since she'd walked out two days ago. She needed to apologize. But not tonight. Tonight she just wanted to run and then sleep.

A car approached from behind, and even though she was on the opposite side of the road, she moved onto the shoulder. The car roared past, a blur of some dark color, then braked. It stood idling. Waiting for her.

There was nothing but plowed fields on either side of the road, broken only by thin stands of trees. No lights were visible, other than the taillights of the car. In just a few minutes, it would be fully dark.

What had she been thinking, to run so far out into the countryside in the evening?

She *hadn't* been thinking. She'd been running away from everything that was complicating her life.

The car door opened and one of the complications stepped out.

"Gideon," she said, slowing to a walk. "What are you doing out here?"

"I was going to ask you the same thing," he said. "It's dark, Zoe. You don't have a reflective vest or a light. What's going on?"

"It wasn't dark when I started running," she said. Okay, that was stupid. She should have been paying attention. She should have turned around two miles ago.

"Yeah, well, it is now. I'll drive you home."

"I'm exercising," she said. "Running is the point."

"Get in the car, Zoe."

Her hackles rose. "I don't take orders from anyone."

"Let me rephrase it, then. Perhaps you haven't

noticed, but you're five miles away from Spruce Lake and you're headed in the wrong direction. Running along the side of the road, you're practically invisible. So either get in the car yourself, or I'll pick you up and dump you in." He waited a beat. "Please."

He was right. She had no business being out here on these deserted roads in the dark. But she didn't like admitting she was wrong. And she *really* didn't like being told what to do. "You think you can catch me?" As she watched him, her heart began thumping in anticipation. "Go ahead and try."

She had no idea he could move so fast.

She'd barely started running when he was on her. He tossed her over his shoulder, clapped one hand on her rear end to steady her, strode to his car and dropped her onto the front seat. Before she could regain her equilibrium, he closed the door and slid behind the wheel.

"You are the most stubborn woman I've ever met."

She jiggled the door handle, infuriated that he'd engaged the childproof locks. "Let me out, Gideon," she said in a low voice.

The car idled as he studied her. "What's wrong?" he asked, his voice gentle.

"You're trying to tell me what to do," she said furiously. "Keeping me in this car against my will. That's what's wrong."

"Besides that. You're an intelligent woman. You know damn well you shouldn't be running out here at night. My God, Zoe! You're even wearing dark clothes."

"There's a fluorescent stripe on my shorts," she shot back, realizing immediately how idiotic she sounded. "Let me out. You can follow me back to town."

"I'll drive you home. It's completely dark now. You might step in a pothole and hurt yourself."

"I don't need someone to tell me what to do," she said, her voice rising. "To make my decisions for me. I've been doing that for a long time."

"I guess I'm saving you from yourself, then," he said. He made a three-point turn and headed toward Spruce Lake.

"Now you're pissing me off, Gideon."

"You're pissing *me* off," he retorted. "You want to do something idiotic just because I told you not to."

"*Told* being the operative word. What gives you the right to tell me to do anything?"

The hum of tires on asphalt was the only noise in the car. Finally Gideon said, "Maybe I think what happened the other night gives me some rights."

"*Rights?* You think that a few kisses and a little petting gives you the right to order me around?"

"Zoe, you're overreacting. I picked you up because you were running in the dark in the middle of nowhere and it wasn't safe. That's all."

His voice was calm and logical. He was right. And it infuriated her. A corona of light in the blackness ahead of them signaled they were approaching Spruce Lake. As soon as they reached the first houses, she said, "Let me out. We're back in civilization."

He glanced at her. "You think I'll just dump you here? What kind of men have you been dating?"

"I haven't been—"

The car swerved. "You don't date?"

"I've been on dates," she said, angry with herself for her slip. Just not more than one or two with anyone.

"But you haven't slept with any of them."

Confiding something in the heat of passion was a lot different than discussing it while sitting in a car, damp with sweat, angry as hell and wondering if her deodorant was holding. "That's none of your business."

"It was my business the other night," he said softly.

"Yeah, well, things change."

He pulled into her driveway and released the lock. She yanked the door open and ran up the steps to her porch.

As she dug her key out of the tiny pocket in the waistband of her shorts, she heard him climbing the stairs behind her.

She'd just managed to open the door when he murmured into her ear, "I don't think we've finished our discussion, Zoe."

CHAPTER FOURTEEN

"OH, WE'RE DONE, Gideon. We are so done." She toed off her running shoes and resisted the impulse to throw them at him. Instead, she lined them up carefully on the mat beside the door.

"Because I was concerned about you?" he said, his voice incredulous. "Because I didn't want you to get hurt?"

"Because you thought you had the right to order me around. You're just like Derrick." She shoved her hands through her damp hair. "He thought he could tell me what to do, too."

"Is that why you shot him, Zoe?" He stepped closer. Into her space. "Because he tried to keep you safe?"

"Safe?" Anger rushed through her, obliterating the last remnants of logic or sanity. "He broke two of my ribs once. Another time he knocked me into a wall and I ended up with a concussion. I lost count of how many black eyes he gave me. Does that sound safe to you?"

"Damn it, Zoe. I wasn't trying to hurt you." He grabbed her shoulders and shook her lightly. "Why don't you understand that? Why is it about power and control? Why can't I just be concerned about you?"

"It's always about power and control," she said. It had started with her father and ended with Derrick. Now she had to be the one in control. And Gideon had just taken that away from her.

It scared the hell out of her.

"Yeah? How's this for control?" he said, yanking her against him and crushing her mouth beneath his.

She tasted his frustration and the fear beneath it, but her body still responded to his touch. Angry at him, angrier at herself, she grabbed his head and deepened the kiss. He wanted control? She'd show him control.

Shoving him against the front door, she twined one leg around him. His arousal throbbed against her, hot even through his jeans and her shorts. She reached between their bodies and caressed him, drinking in his moan.

Suddenly he picked her up and laid her on the floor. Shoving one leg between hers, he kissed her frantically as he tugged on her T-shirt. He broke the kiss as he pulled it over her head, then fastened his mouth to hers again as he yanked up her sports bra.

She arched into his hands as he caressed her. There was no gentleness in his touch, only a fierce desperation that fueled her uncontrollable desire. She needed him inside her. Now.

She was shaking too much to unbutton the unyielding denim. He pushed her fingers away and sat up long enough to shuck the jeans and his boxers and unbutton his flannel shirt. She tossed her sports bra away and tugged off her shorts. He slipped on a condom and surged into her.

She rolled them both until she was on top of him. He covered her breasts with his hands as she rode him, tension winding more and more tightly inside her. Suddenly she exploded, release crashing through her. His groan as he followed her seemed far-off and distant.

He drew her down against his chest, tucking her head beneath his chin. He held her tightly for a moment, then began stroking her back. His hand was steady and gentle. Calming. As if he was comforting her.

My God, what had she done?

She tried to break away, but he held her more tightly. "No," he said. "Let me hold you for a minute."

She didn't want to be held. She wanted to run into her room, lock the door and stay there until he was gone. She'd wanted to be in control, and she had been. Now she felt shattered. As if she'd taken something precious and broken it irreparably.

"Not exactly how I'd imagined the first time we made love," he murmured.

"We didn't make love," she said, ashamed of herself. "We had a power struggle and sex was the weapon. I'm sorry, Gideon."

"I'm sorry, too," he said, stroking her back again. He eased away from her. "You can make it up to me." His mouth curved in a tiny smile. "Might take a while, though."

Beneath his teasing words she saw pain in his eyes. He had a right to be hurt.

Standing up, she reached for her clothes, pulling them on without looking at him. She heard him dressing, too.

She expected him to leave, but instead, he came up behind her and put his hands on her shoulders. "You want to tell me what that was all about?"

"It was about sex," she said, her voice flat.

"No, it wasn't. It was about control." He turned her around to look at him. "Want to tell me why?"

"I told you why. Derrick controlled me. I swore I wouldn't ever let that happen again."

"Then I locked you in my car, and you weren't in control anymore." He cupped her face in his hand and brushed his thumb over her cheek. "Do you want to talk about why you were running like the devil was chasing you?"

She was shocked to realize that she did. "Family stuff," she said.

"Yeah?"

He didn't push, and she sank onto the couch and pulled her afghan over her shoulders. She was so cold. "I had a fight with my sisters. They think I'm always telling them what to do."

"*Do* you?" He sat down next to her and put an arm around her.

She wouldn't let herself lean into him. But she wanted to. "I can't stop myself from pointing it out when they do foolish things."

"What *you* consider foolish things."

"I suppose so. It's hard, you know? When you think they're going to get hurt." He'd just done the same thing to her, and she'd gone crazy.

"Tell me about it," he said as she burrowed more deeply into the afghan. He smoothed a hand over her hair. "Do they point out foolish things *you've* done?"

"Yeah." She sighed. "They're going to have a field day when they hear about this."

"You're going to tell them?"

"They'll know something is wrong." She tried to smile. "Triplet ESP rears its ugly head."

"Is that what the fight was about? Me?" He frowned. "I don't want to come between you and your sisters."

"It wasn't about you. It was about something Bree didn't do. And about Fiona's life in general." But the truth was, it was about their father and the scars he'd caused. She wasn't sure she wanted to tell him about John Henry.

"It started with my father," she found herself saying. "He was a professor at Collier College. An English professor. He won the Pulitzer for fiction when I was a kid, and suddenly he was a celebrity. Turned out he liked being a star.

"He'd always been possessive and jealous of us, but it got worse after that. He needed constant adulation and expected my sisters and me and our mother to provide it. He told us constantly we didn't love him enough, that we didn't care what happened to him. If we wanted to spend a day with a friend, he'd pout. He'd say we liked our friends better than we liked him. After Mom died and it was just Dad and us, it got really bad. We fought all the time."

"I'm sorry," he said, stroking her shoulder. "No wonder you always need to be in control."

"That's why I married Derrick. I was desperate to get out of the house. To get my life back." She sighed as she leaned her head against the couch. "Pretty ironic, huh? Derrick turned out to be just like my dad. Possessive. Demanding. Abusive."

His hand tensed on her shoulder. "Your dad hit you?"

"No. He never touched us. It was all mind games and manipulating us emotionally."

"Sounds like your father pitted you and your sisters against each other."

"Yes. So of course we fought."

"And you're still fighting. Hard to break old habits," he said.

"It is." She sighed. "I need to apologize to them. I've been putting it off."

"And that's why you were out running? So you wouldn't have to apologize?"

"I guess so."

"You're lucky you have your sisters. I wish I had some siblings."

She jumped up and stared out the window, feeling as if he'd just punched her in the gut. "Do you want me to tell you I'm sorry I killed your brother, Gideon? I *am* sorry. I shot and killed my husband, and that's a burden I'll carry for the rest of my life. But I had no choice. If I hadn't stopped him, he would have killed me."

"Zoe, it's okay. I didn't mean it that way." He came up behind her and closed his hands over her stiff shoulders. "I wasn't talking about Derrick. I don't want to talk about him tonight. I meant, I wished my mother and stepfather had had more kids. That I had a normal family."

He stroked her arms, comforting her, and the vise around her heart eased a little. "Is there such a thing?"

"Yes," he said with conviction. "There is. My mother and I were close. And we had a normal relationship."

"How do you define normal?" she said.

"Typical teenage rebellion," he said with a laugh, "and my mom trying to protect me from doing stupid things, me trying to do as many stupid things as possible." He moved away from her. "But she loved me and I loved her. I was always clear on that."

"When did she pass away?" Zoe asked, turning around.

"Three years ago. She had cancer."

"I'm sorry."

"Yeah, me, too." He stared down at his hands. "Truth? That's one of the reasons I came back when my father had his stroke. I was feeling adrift. Alone. I guess I was looking to reconnect with him."

"Have you?"

"No." He sighed. "He doesn't want me here."

"I'm sorry, Gideon…"

"It's the stroke. He's helpless, and he hates that I'm seeing him that way."

"How's he doing? Is he getting any better?"

"Yeah, there's been a lot of improvement. He can talk now, although it's slow and hard to understand. He can sit up by himself. The therapist told me she's going to have him on his feet in a day or two and get him moving again."

"So you'll put him into rehab, then go back to Milwaukee?" she asked. Was that what she wanted? For Gideon to leave?

She wasn't sure. And that was scary.

"That's the plan."

"He's lucky you were able to stay this long."

He shrugged. "Whatever kind of relationship we had, he's my father." Gideon said it casually, as if everyone felt that way about their parents. As if everyone accepted responsibility so easily.

Gideon was nothing like Derrick.

The thought popped into her head out of the blue, and she knew it was true. Derrick had never thought of anyone but himself.

"Wallace doesn't deserve you," she said.

"No matter what, he's blood," Gideon said. "Bottom line."

He stood up. "Are you feeling better now?"

"Yes. Thanks for sticking around to talk." She drew the afghan more tightly around herself.

"This has been an unsettling evening."

She nodded, then rose to face him. "Good night, Gideon."

She stood at the window, watching his car pull out

of her driveway. Who had the power in their relationship now?

She wasn't sure. She wasn't even sure if it was important.

That was the scariest thing of all.

"ANYBODY HOME?" Zoe called, walking into the kitchen of their father's house.

"In the living room," Fiona answered.

Zoe found her sorting through a box of old clothes. Girls' old clothes. Three of each outfit, all identical. The sight brought back memories of their father and the fights they'd had about dressing alike. Ugly, painful fights.

"I didn't know he kept all this stuff," Zoe said.

"Apparently he did."

Zoe dropped to the floor next to her sister. "You should have waited. I would have helped you."

Fiona looked up from where she sat, cross-legged, on the shabby, dark green carpet. "You were supposed to be working, and I had nothing better to do."

"No fabulous jewelry to design?" Zoe said with a smile.

Fiona lifted a pair of child-size corduroy overalls out of the box. "I'm not sure what I want to work on."

Zoe touched her sister's shoulder. "I'm sorry, Fee. For what I said the other night. You're entitled to live your life the way you want. I shouldn't have criticized you."

Fiona carefully folded the overalls. "That's never stopped you before."

"Maybe I've realized that always being in control isn't necessarily a good thing."

"There's a breakthrough," Fiona said, finally looking at her.

Zoe pulled a small dress out of the box. "I remember this."

"Are you trying to change the subject?" Fiona asked. She leaned closer to Zoe and peered at her face. "What happened to cause this sudden insight of yours?"

"Nothing I want to talk about," Zoe said. She couldn't bring herself to tell her sister what had happened the night before. She was still too ashamed of herself.

"Aren't you the one always telling us we need to talk about stuff? To deal with it?"

"Not everything needs to be dissected and discussed." At least not when it was this painful.

"So it's okay to do the social-worker thing to us, but we can't do it to you?"

"I'm a trained professional," Zoe said, trying to lighten the conversation. "Haven't you ever heard 'Don't try this at home'?"

Fiona folded another dress. "So why aren't you at work today? No women at the shelter?"

Thank goodness Fee was letting it go. "There are always women at the shelter," Zoe answered. "But I wanted to see you and Bree. I didn't like the way we left things."

"Nothing new there."

"I know. But I want to change that. Dad is gone. Maybe we need to stop looking for a hidden meaning in everything someone else says." She took a deep breath and poked at the identical dresses with her toe. "I want to stop fighting with you and Bree."

"Is that all you want?" Fiona said, her voice wistful. "To stop fighting?"

Zoe wanted to be close to her sisters. To feel that tight bond, holding them together no matter what. Was it still possible? "What do you want, Fee?"

"I don't know." Fiona stood up and began to replace the clothes in the box. "I have no idea what would make me happy."

"I thought your jewelry made you happy," Zoe said, lifting the soft piles of children's clothes and arranging them in the box. "When we were kids, you could work on your jewelry for hours."

"I'm not sure what I want to do next," Fiona said. "My manager is pushing me to concentrate on the FeeMac designs. But I have other ideas, things that wouldn't work for the brand."

Fiona hadn't opened up this much in a long time. Zoe tried not to overreact. "Why not work on your new ideas while you're in Spruce Lake?" she said. "Think of it as bonus time. You probably wouldn't be working on FeeMac, anyway."

"I don't have a studio," Fiona said.

"Use the garage. You and Bree can park your cars in the driveway."

Fiona stuffed the last of the clothes back in the box and stood up. "I'll think about it," she said. But there was a new sparkle in her eyes.

Before Zoe could answer, she heard the back door slam. "Sounds like Bree's home."

She met her sister in the hall. "Hey, Bree."

Bree dropped her briefcase on the old marble-topped hall table. "Zo. What are you doing here in the middle of the day?"

"I wanted to see you and Fee. I'm sorry I got on you

about the job at the high school," she said. "I had no right to do that, and I'll try not to do it again."

Bree studied her for a moment. "Can I put money on that? Because I think I'd make a bundle." There was no malice in her voice. Just weary acceptance. "I know you're doing it because you care about me and Charlie."

"I do, but that's no excuse."

"Fair enough. We'll put it behind us." She started up the stairs. "I heard something at school today. Something I think you should know."

"Yeah?" Zoe and Fiona followed Bree up to her room. Zoe sat on the tattered chair that had always been there. The floral print was faded and the arms were worn. A spring poked through the cushion. But its familiarity was oddly comforting.

Bree dropped onto the bed and Fiona lounged in the doorway. "I overheard a couple of the staff talking," she said. "It sounds as if Barb Johnson is having an affair with one of the other teachers."

"What?" Zoe said, shocked.

"Get out of here," Fiona said.

"They used to leave together every day at lunch."

"That's not proof they're having an affair," Zoe said, trying to recover. "Teachers probably go to lunch together all the time."

"Yeah, a bunch went out today in a big group. But this guy and Barb always went alone. And one of the women saw them together the other night."

Zoe frowned. "Barb's been in the shelter for more than two weeks."

"She doesn't go out?" Bree asked. "Ever?"

"Not during the day," Zoe answered.

"What about at night?"

"I don't think so."

Fiona stepped into the room and joined Bree on the bed. "Maybe you better find out."

CHAPTER FIFTEEN

"HI, DAD," Gideon said as he walked into his father's hospital room. "How are you feeling today?"

"Like…shit." Wallace scowled at him and dropped the sandwich he'd been holding. From the smears of mayonnaise on his cheek, Gideon saw he'd been having trouble eating it.

Gideon opened the napkin and managed to wipe most of the mess off his father's face before Wallace jerked away. "You need some help with that? I can call one of the nurses," Gideon said, carefully not meeting his father's eyes. He didn't want Wallace to see the pity in them.

"No."

Wallace's favorite word.

"How about a visitor?" Gideon said. "I brought Sally Beckman by. You said you wanted to see her."

"No." Wallace shoved away the remains of his lunch.

"I'll have one of the nurses clean that up. Sally and I will wait in the lounge."

Gideon walked out of the room without waiting for an answer. His father had asked to see Sally, and Gideon had finally managed to get hold of her. At first she'd seemed surprised Wallace wanted her to visit. When Gideon had assured her Wallace had asked to see her, she'd been pleased and flustered.

"He's finishing lunch," Gideon said as he led her toward the tiny waiting room. "I told him we'd stay here until he's done."

"I don't want to interrupt his meal," Sally said, smoothing the skirt of her dress. "Maybe I should come back another time."

"It won't take long," Gideon assured her. "Unless you have to be somewhere?"

"No, not today. But I don't want to upset him. Wallace likes his meals at regular times."

"He's on the hospital schedule now," Gideon said, steering Sally toward one of the ugly upholstered chairs. "He has to eat when they bring him his food."

Sally shook her head. "I'll bet poor Wallace doesn't like that."

"Poor Wallace" didn't like anything about his hospital stay. But then, Gideon admitted, dealing with a stroke was horrible. In one moment, Wallace had gone from a vital, self-sufficient man to a helpless one.

"He's having a hard time," Gideon said.

"It's good of you to stay here with him," Sally said.

"He's my father."

He studied Sally out of the corner of his eye. She wasn't at all the kind of woman he'd imagined would interest his father. She had a bland, heavily made-up face and wore drab clothes. Her blond hair was as faded as her blue eyes. She was a little overweight and seemed to blend into the wallpaper.

Gideon had assumed a man like his father, someone powerful and confident, would want a woman who was equally strong. Sally Beckman seemed the exact opposite.

But hey, whatever floated your boat.

A picture of Zoe on the couch beneath him, naked to

the waist, her face flushed with passion, materialized in his mind. Followed by the memory of her riding him a few nights ago.

Strong, assertive women apparently did it for him.

He refused to consider that it was Zoe specifically he wanted.

He cleared his throat. "So, Sally, where did you meet Wallace?"

"I work at the drugstore. Wallace and I would talk whenever he came in." She blushed. "One day he asked me to go to dinner with him."

"And it's been happily ever after since then, right?" Gideon smiled encouragingly at Sally.

"Of course," she said, but she looked away quickly.

Before he could ask Sally anything else, one of the nurses stuck her head into the lounge. "Your father is done with his lunch," the young woman said. *And cleaned up,* she mouthed silently.

"Thanks, Bella," he said easily before turning to Sally. "Ready for a visit?"

She fiddled with the handle of her purse. "Will I…um… Can he talk?"

"You won't be able to have a regular conversation with him," Gideon said, taking her hand. "He'll understand you and he can speak, but it takes a while. Talk to him normally, be patient when he answers, and you'll do fine."

"Okay," she said nervously. "Let's go see him."

Ten minutes later Gideon stood across his father's bed from Sally, wondering how fast he could get the woman out of Wallace's room. She was twisting her hands together and couldn't seem to look directly at the old man. She'd started out fine, telling him about mutual friends and sharing some gossip, but she'd faltered and finally stopped talking altogether. As Wallace became increasingly agitated, she retreated from the bed.

It was obvious Wallace hated having Sally see him struggling. His words were becoming more garbled, and his hands moved restlessly on the blanket.

Gideon stepped to the end of the bed, wondering how to end this fiasco. As he stood poised to intervene, he heard the tap of high heels in the corridor outside the room.

They slowed, then stopped at the door, and Zoe stood there uncertainly.

He hurried out the door and took her hand, tugging her toward the room as if she was a lifeline. "I brought his friend to visit," he whispered, "and it's a disaster. Help me get her out of here."

Understanding filled her eyes, and she nodded. Thank God Zoe was so quick.

As she entered the room, Zoe stopped at the foot of the bed. "Hello, Wallace," she said softly. "I hear you're doing better. I'm glad."

Wallace tried to speak, but only meaningless sounds came out of his mouth. He gestured angrily with his arm and almost knocked the water pitcher off his bed table. Zoe's fingers tightened on the strap of her briefcase.

"My father's friend Sally Beckman came to visit," Gideon said.

Zoe stiffened. "Sally! What are you doing here?"

"I was visiting Wallace." She fiddled with her purse, not looking at any of them. "Gideon told me Wallace wanted to see me."

"I can't believe you're here," Zoe said, dropping her briefcase to the floor. "Have you forgotten everything we talked about?"

Wallace was struggling to get out of bed, and Gideon

laid a hand on Zoe's arm. "Maybe you better leave. You're upsetting my father."

"Sally, please come with me," Zoe said, reaching for the other woman as if to physically remove her.

Sally had moved closer to the bed, and Wallace clamped his hand around Sally's wrist. The woman recoiled as if he'd hit her. As she tried to pull away, Wallace held on.

"Let her go, Wallace," Zoe said sharply. "Right now."

Sally stood frozen, her gaze darting from Zoe to Wallace.

Nausea churned in Gideon's stomach as he watched Sally. He recognized that look. The frozen fear, the inability to make a decision. The reluctance to disobey a man.

He'd seen it in too many of the women who came through his office. Women who were the victims of domestic violence.

He'd seen it in Zoe, too. Sickness filled his mouth with bile. The first time he'd seen her, in that jail cell, she'd flinched when he made a sudden move in her direction.

"Wait in the hall, Zoe," he said quietly. "I'll bring Sally out."

Zoe turned to Wallace, her eyes blazing. Then, without a word, she picked up her briefcase and stormed out of the room.

Gideon walked over to Sally and pried his father's fingers off her wrist. "Come on," he said gently. "I think we've spent enough time here." He didn't look at his father as he led Sally out of the room.

Zoe was pacing the hall, and she spun around as they emerged. "Sally, what were you thinking?"

Sally's mouth trembled. "He wanted to see me, Zoe. I thought... I thought it would be a kind thing to do."

"There is no kindness for a man like Wallace," Zoe answered. "His sort think it's weakness." She shoved her hands through her hair. "I thought you agreed you wouldn't see him anymore."

"He was so nice to me right before he got sick," Sally said, her voice wistful. "He even brought me a box of candy. From my favorite store in Green Bay. That's a long drive. He went there because he knew I liked it."

"Sally..." Zoe began, but Gideon stepped between them. Sally needed comforting right now, not criticism.

"Let's go into the lounge," he said. "Where we'll have a little more privacy."

Zoe transfered her gaze from Sally to Gideon.

My God. He'd never seen this side of Zoe. No wonder Dave was nervous about her. She looked as if she was ready to ride into battle. All that was missing was a sword and a shield.

"Back off, Gideon," she said.

Most men would run from that look, those eyes. He stepped closer, fascinated.

"Let's take this into the lounge," he repeated. "You're upsetting Sally."

The older woman was crying softly, tears streaking her makeup. Zoe looked at her and took a deep, shuddering breath. "Come on, Sally," she said, the warrior gone as if she'd never been. "Let's go sit down."

She placed an arm around Sally's shoulders and steered her into the lounge, then eased her onto a couch. Zoe sat next to her, pulling a tissue from her briefcase. Sally held it over her face.

"I shouldn't have lost my temper with you, Sally." Zoe brushed a strand of hair away from the older woman's face. "You're the victim, not the problem."

"You were right," Sally sobbed. "I shouldn't have come to visit him. But I thought he'd changed."

"I know," Zoe said, pulling Sally close and wrapping her arms around her. "I know."

Gideon sat on one of the stiff, uncomfortable chairs and watched the two women. As Sally cried in her arms, Zoe kept handing her tissues, kept murmuring to her. Finally Sally pushed away.

"I'm so stupid," Sally said.

"No, you're not." Zoe took Sally's hands. "You're not stupid, Sally. You're a wonderful woman trying to do a nice thing for a man who doesn't deserve it. That's all."

Sally shook her head. "You're right, Zoe. I had no business coming here."

"What's this all about?" Gideon asked.

Zoe blotted Sally's cheek, then turned her toward Gideon. Her makeup was gone, and the left side of her face was dark yellow with splotches of purple. The skin around her left eye was yellow, as well.

He stared at Sally, unable to believe what he was seeing. "Those are old bruises," he finally said.

"Yes." Zoe put her arm around Sally's shoulders. "Any guesses where she got them?"

"Wallace did that?" Horrified, he looked from Zoe to Sally. Sally nodded slowly.

"My father hit you?" he demanded.

Sally nodded again, then bit her lip. "I'd like to go home," she said to Zoe.

"Do you want me to call your friend Carrie to come get you?" Zoe asked.

"I'll be fine," Sally said.

Zoe smiled. "I know you will. But Carrie has been

so worried about you. It would make her feel better to have something to do. Why don't you let me call her?"

"Okay." Sally slumped against the back of the couch like a puppet whose strings had been suddenly cut.

Zoe opened her cell phone. She turned away and began talking. Gideon heard her say Sally's name and the hospital. Finally she closed the phone. "Carrie's on her way," she said. "Do you want to wait for her here, or do you want to go stand by the front door?"

"I'll wait by the door." Sally stumbled to her feet and swayed for a moment, and Zoe held on to her.

"I'll walk you down and wait until she gets here."

Gideon stood up. "I'm sorry, Sally." He felt totally inadequate. What did you say to a woman who'd been beaten by your father?

"It's not your fault, Gideon," she answered with a sweet smile. "You didn't know."

I should have, he thought as he watched the women leave. He remembered how his mother had flinched at sudden, loud noises. How her hands shook, even after she realized what the noises were.

How she'd fought when Wallace had tried to get more custodial visits with Gideon.

How she'd moved them to Milwaukee, even though she had a good job in Spruce Lake and all her friends were here.

She'd tried her best to keep him away from Wallace. He should have put two and two together.

Wallace had beaten his mother. Just as he'd probably beaten Derrick's mother.

And Derrick had beaten Zoe. He'd learned how to treat women from his father.

Zoe hadn't been lying. She *had* been protecting

herself when she shot his brother. Gideon kicked one of the ugly chairs. Why hadn't he seen that? Why had he been so blind?

He leaped to his feet and hurried to Wallace's room. His father was lying on the bed, staring at the wall.

"I know what you did to Sally," Gideon said. "I saw the bruises on her face."

Wallace sneered at him. "You kn...nothing," he managed to say.

"Yeah, Dad, I do." Gideon clenched his hands into fists and shoved them into his pockets. "You hit my mother, didn't you?" He felt a jolt of satisfaction when Wallace looked away. "Derrick's mother, too. Was the car crash that killed her an accident? Or didn't she see any other way out?

"And Derrick." Gideon slapped the rail at the foot of the bed. "What did you do to him?"

Wallace tried to answer. No doubt wanted to give justification. Excuses.

There were no excuses. "No wonder you hate Zoe. She fought back. She didn't allow Derrick to treat her that way. And you've never been able to control her."

He paced the room, unable to look at the figure on the bed. "My God. I have no idea who you are, Wallace." He couldn't call the man his father. What would that make Gideon? A monster's son? "I'm not sure I want to know."

He headed for the door. "I have to leave." He didn't look back as he headed for the stairs.

CHAPTER SIXTEEN

ZOE STOOD on the front porch of Wallace's home and rubbed damp palms down her jeans. Gideon's car was in the driveway. There was a light on in the kitchen. She had no excuse to run away.

She rang the doorbell once. Tentatively. As if she hoped he wouldn't hear it.

She closed her eyes and reached for it again. It had been a long time since she'd thought of herself as a coward.

Pressing the doorbell, she listened to its insistent ring echo off the walls. She shouldn't have waited to come to Gideon. She should have been here the day after their last evening together. Now, after what had happened at the hospital today, she wasn't leaving without talking to him.

Finally the door opened. Gideon was shirtless and wore the same baggy shorts he'd been wearing the last time she'd come to the house. His fingers looked red and scraped. As if he'd been punching the bag bare-handed. His face was haggard and he held a glass of amber liquid. "What do you want, Zoe?"

"To talk to you. May I come in?"

"God, no." His voice filled with revulsion, and she jerked back as if he'd struck her. She had expected him to be angry, but not like this. Was it because of how she'd treated him that night? Or was it the ugly truths she'd forced him to face? The reality he now had to acknowledge?

Funny that she'd come here to comfort him. That she'd thought he'd *want* her comfort.

"Why not?" she managed to ask in a calm voice.

He rubbed his hand over his face, and in the silence she heard the faint rasp of his beard. "There's nothing in this house but hatred and cruelty," he said. "You don't belong here, Zoe."

"*You're* here, Gideon," she said, eyeing the glass in his hand. How much had he drunk? "I didn't come to see the house. I'm here to see you."

"You were right. About everything." He took a swallow. "About Wallace. About Derrick. God, you must hate the name Tate."

She stepped inside and pushed him gently backward. Into the house. "I don't hate everyone named Tate."

"I didn't believe you, you know. I thought you'd exaggerated. Lied. That you'd gotten away with murder." He threw the glass against the wall. It slid down and landed on the wood floor with a dull thud, and the ice cubes skated across the floor. "I was angry at myself for wanting you."

"I understand. I didn't want to be attracted to you, either. But that was before you knew me, or I knew you. You believe me now, don't you?"

"Hell, yes. I'd kill Derrick myself if he wasn't already dead."

"No, you wouldn't," she said, picking up the glass and setting it on the hall table. "You couldn't kill anyone."

His eyes darkened as he stared at her. "Shows what you know, Zoe. He hurt you."

Her heart fluttered. "And you're making it better," she whispered.

As she spoke, he punched his fist into the wall above the table, leaving a small indentation. "Damn it!"

He hadn't heard her. It was probably just as well. She closed the door behind her and inhaled slowly to steady herself. The house smelled faintly of decay and deterioration, and the ghosts closed in on her.

Derrick yelling. Raising his hand.

Wallace shredding her with well-chosen, cutting words.

All the women Wallace had abused watching her. Asking why there hadn't been justice for them.

She stared down the ghosts until they faded away. "Let's go sit," she said. "Talk."

"No. I don't want you in this house. I don't want to think about you here."

"It's just a house, Gideon, that's all." Brave words from someone who could barely bring herself to walk through the front door.

"I hate this place," he said. "I always have."

"Then let's go somewhere else."

"Why do you want to spend time with me? Why did you come looking for me?"

She grabbed his shoulders and shook him. "Snap out of it, Gideon. You're not your father or your brother. You can't take the blame for what they did." She shook him again. "How much have you had to drink?"

"Not as much as I need," he said.

"Okay. Let's go." She grabbed his hand and towed him toward the door.

"Hold on, Zoe." He pulled away from her and gazed at her. His eyes cleared. "Let me take a shower and get cleaned up. Okay?"

"All right. I'll wait in the car." She watched him disappear up the stairs and waited until she heard the water running. Then she retreated to her car.

Fifteen minutes later Gideon came out of the house, his hair still damp. He'd exchanged the shorts for jeans and a red shirt, and Zoe found herself watching his long-legged, easy gait.

He'd also sobered up. "Sorry, Zoe," he said as he got in the car. "I made a fool of myself, didn't I?"

"No, you didn't." She pulled away from the house too fast. "You have every right to be upset."

"Yeah. Stupid way to handle it, though. Good thing you got here when you did. I was halfway to shit-faced."

"I noticed," she said. "You want something to eat? To take the edge off the whiskey?"

"Nope. Cold shower did that."

"Okay." She turned onto the main road out of town and drove until she reached the entrance of a county park, where she pulled into the parking lot.

"What's this?" Gideon asked. "What are we doing here?"

The smell of Wallace's house clung to her, and she needed to get rid of it. "I thought we could both use some fresh air."

"Yeah." He rubbed at the backs of his hands, which were still red. "Fresh air is good."

"It's going to be dark soon," she said. "Let's walk."

They hiked down a gravel path that wound its way through a stand of white pines. The soft needles brushed her arm and the scent of pine resin filled the air. The air was cooling rapidly as the sun set, and she was glad she'd worn her thick fisherman's sweater.

The pines were giving way to maples and oaks when

Gideon slowed and looked at her. "Why did you come to my house, Zoe?"

"I should have been there a lot sooner. Right after I...used you." She lifted a clump of old leaf debris with the toe of her boot. "I was a coward. I didn't know what to say to you."

"So why tonight?"

"You know why." She pushed her hands deep into her pockets. Maybe he wanted nothing more to do with her. "I saw how upset you were about what happened at the hospital. I thought you might want someone to talk to." She kicked at more dead leaves. "I guess I hoped I could make up for what I did the other night."

"There's nothing to make up for."

"Yes, there is. What I did was ugly. And wrong."

"Maybe that evens out what my family has done to you."

"You have no part in what your father or your brother did. None at all."

He smoothed one finger over her cheek. "I was a jerk when you came to the door."

"I didn't take it personally," she said.

"Thank God." He touched her mouth. "I'm glad you came to me."

"No one should have to deal with that kind of revelation alone."

He took her hand and glanced around the shadowed woods. "Why did you bring me to this park?"

"When I was a kid, I used to ride my bike out here when things got...hard at home." She touched the curling bark of a birch tree. "The exercise probably helped as much as anything."

It had been more than the exercise. This was where

she'd come when the world was collapsing around her—when her father was unbearable, when she and her sisters were fighting. Her refuge. The place where she'd constructed fantasies about happy families.

And now she'd brought Gideon here.

She held his hand more tightly. Maybe he could find a little of the peace she'd found here.

"So if I look closely, will I see the ghosts of you and your sisters playing in the trees?" he asked.

She tugged her hand away. "I came here alone."

"Your family didn't win any prizes, either, did it?" he said quietly.

"No. But we're not talking about my family today. We're talking about yours."

He stared into the woods. "Nothing is what I thought it was," he said abruptly. "Wallace, Derrick, the years I spent in Spruce Lake as a kid—it all feels like smoke and mirrors. Like an illusion I never even suspected was false."

"Don't be so hard on yourself. You were twelve when you left, Gideon. Twelve-year-old boys are pretty oblivious to what's going on around them." Her nephew, Charlie, was a perfect example—he was too absorbed in his studies and his snakes to notice anything else.

"I came here thinking I could reconnect with Wallace," he said. He slapped the trunk of a maple tree. "He's my father. He's part of me, and I thought we should have a relationship."

"That's pretty generous, considering what he did when you were a kid."

"I want nothing to do with him now."

Damp cold penetrated her sweater, and she looked at

Gideon. His shirt was just thin cotton. "Let's head back to the car. It's getting chilly."

They retraced their steps as night closed in on the forest. By the time they reached Zoe's car, it was almost completely dark. An owl hooted in the distance and some small creature scampered through the undergrowth. Zoe put the key into the ignition, but before she could turn it, Gideon put his hand on hers.

"How did you know this was exactly what I needed? To come out here, to talk to you."

"I didn't," she said. "But I didn't want you to be alone after what happened today." They sat close together in her small car, the gearshift the only thing separating them. Gideon's scent filled the air, and she touched his cheek. "I saw how devastated you were when you realized what had happened to Sally. To her face."

He took her hand. "When I was hitting the body bag tonight, I was thinking of you, Zoe. Of how Derrick marked you. I couldn't bear it."

He leaned over and kissed her, brushing his lips over hers lightly, a gentle touch that held no heat. As if he was afraid she'd break if he really kissed her.

As if he was afraid she'd think of Derrick and what he'd done.

As he began to ease away from her, she grabbed his head and kissed him back. He froze for a moment, then he answered her desire with his own. His mouth moved over hers, but she felt him holding back. Hesitating.

No doubt remembering the other night, when she'd been so desperate to be in control.

Control wouldn't be an issue tonight, she promised herself. This would just be fun. Playful.

When he opened his mouth, she let him in, stroking

his tongue with hers, tasting him. He groaned as he teased her lower lip, sucked it into his mouth, nibbled on it.

He tried to pull her closer, but the gearshift was in the way. Without breaking the connection of their mouths, she climbed over and sat on his lap. His erection burned into her and she squirmed against him.

"Zoe," he said, his breathing ragged in the silence of the car. "Are you sure about this?"

She took his hands and put them on her breasts, and he surged against her. His fingers danced over her curves, testing the weight, caressing her. Even through her thick sweater she felt their heat. "I'm sure, Gideon. Can we forget about the other night and just have fun?"

"Is that what you want, Zoe? Fun?" He circled her nipples with his thumbs.

"Mmm." She sucked on his earlobe, every part of her throbbing. More turned on than she'd ever been in her life. "I want to neck in a parked car like teenagers."

"I think I can get into that game," he murmured. "As long as you know what you're doing."

She dragged her mouth over his and said against his lips, "I have no idea what I'm doing. I've never parked before." He brushed her nipples and she arched into his touch. "I'm hoping you know how to play this game." She pressed herself more tightly against his erection. "Is that okay?" She slid her hands beneath his sweater and touched his hot skin. "Or am I being too forward?"

"I think I can keep up with you." He threaded his fingers through her hair and smiled at her. "You want to play games, that's fine with me."

She wanted him with a wildness, an abandon she'd never felt before. She wanted his hands on her, and she wanted to touch him. She wanted to feel his skin against hers. Holding his gaze, she fumbled with the button of his jeans. "Yeah, I want to play games."

His zipper stuck, and she caressed the hard length of him beneath it. He shoved her sweater to her chin, then cupped her breasts again. "It's too dark in here," he whispered. "I want to see you."

"I want to see you, too," she said, tugging at the zipper again.

"Hold on." He pulled her hands away and kissed one palm, then the other. "Me first."

He reached behind her and unhooked her bra, then pulled her sweater over her head. As he drew her bra down her arms, moonlight splashed over her. "Even more beautiful than I remembered," he whispered. He put his hands over her breasts. "When you neck in a car, it's traditional for the guy to try to sweet-talk the girl into the backseat." He took one nipple into his mouth and suckled her. "How am I doing?"

"Keep talking," she gasped. He unbuttoned her jeans and shoved them down her hips with her panties, and kicked one leg off. She held her breath as he slid his finger over her.

"You're definitely on the right track," she managed to say, reaching between them to touch his hard length. He groaned and lifted to meet her.

He let her go, raised his hips and pushed his own jeans down, grabbing a foil wrapper from his pocket. She took it out of his hands and put the condom on him, then kissed him hungrily.

He slid inside her, holding her hips as he began to move. Sensation washed through her, drenching her with pleasure. "Gideon," she whispered.

He swirled his tongue around one nipple, then the other. "Backseat?" he muttered.

"Not yet," she cried, tension coiling inside her. "Don't stop, Gideon. Please!"

"Can't stop," he panted, thrusting harder.

Wave after wave of release washed through her. Dimly, she heard someone scream and realized it was her. Gideon tensed, then groaned her name and thrust one more time.

Boneless, she collapsed against his chest and he wrapped his arms around her. He was rubbing his cheek against hers when there was a sharp rapping at the window.

She shot upright and clapped her hands over her breasts until she realized that the windows were completely fogged over. Thank God.

Gideon lifted her off him and turned her around on his lap. She kicked off her panties, which were hanging around one ankle, and yanked up her jeans. As she scrambled over the gearshift, he handed her her sweater and fastened his own jeans.

"Open up," a voice outside the car said.

Zoe dragged her sweater over her head, ignoring the way the wool brushed against her still-aroused nipples. Gideon stuffed her bra beneath his thigh. Taking a deep breath, she rolled the window down.

"What's going… Zoe?" Jamie Evans said incredulously.

"Hello, Jamie," Zoe managed to say. Was it possible to die from embarrassment?

"What the hell are you doing out here?" Jamie asked.

"This is Gideon Tate," she said to Jamie. "You remember him from the shelter the other night, don't you?"

Gideon leaned over her. "Aren't you a little outside your jurisdiction, Jamie? This park is quite a ways from Spruce Lake."

"We patrol the park as a favor to the county," he said, assessing Gideon. He switched his attention to Zoe. "Are you all right?" he asked. "I thought I heard someone scream."

Zoe's cheeks burned. "I'm fine, Jamie. Gideon and I were just talking."

Jamie's gaze traveled over her. Her face was flushed and her hair had to be mussed. She was sure he could see that she wasn't wearing a bra. She hoped he hadn't spotted her panties on the floor of the car.

"Why don't you take this conversation home, Zoe?" he finally said.

"We'll do that," she said, reaching for the ignition key. "I'll see you later, Jamie."

"Yeah. You might want to do your talking in private from now on."

She narrowed her eyes at him. "At least I talk to people. You and Helen ought to have a few chats," she shot back.

"Leave Helen out of this," he said, scowling.

"Then don't get all cute with me."

She rolled up her window and listened to Jamie's squad car drive away.

"Well," she said brightly. "That was humiliating."

"Actually, it was kind of funny," Gideon said with a grin. "Especially the way you went after him there at the end."

"Jamie's never going to let me forget this," she muttered. "I thought I'd better make a preemptive strike."

"I guess I forgot to mention one of the other thrills of necking in a car." He leaned over and kissed her.

"Getting caught." He twined a strand of her hair around his finger. "This is still your game, sweetheart. Do you want another thrill?"

"I think I've had enough excitement for one night," she said.

CHAPTER SEVENTEEN

BY THE TIME they reached Gideon's driveway, Zoe's hands were clamped tightly on the steering wheel. What was going to happen?

What did she want to happen?

Did she want to take Gideon to her bed? Ask him to spend the night?

They'd gotten carried away at the park. What was supposed to be a little harmless necking, nothing more than a game, had turned into lovemaking. Extremely sexy, intense lovemaking, but still a "heat of the moment" thing. Her hormones had been doing the thinking. Gideon's, too, apparently.

Now she had to make a decision that she couldn't blame on hormones. She had to figure out if she wanted Gideon enough to ask him to stay.

She needed to see if she had the courage to reach out and take what she wanted.

The car idling, she said, "So. Here we are. Back where we started." She stared straight ahead.

"Not exactly," he said softly.

"Do you want to come back to my house?" she blurted before she could chicken out.

"What are you asking me, Zoe?"

Finally she looked at him. "What do you think I'm asking?"

"I hope you're asking me to spend the night with you." He pried her hand off the steering wheel and kissed her palm. "I'd like to be boring and conventional and make love with you in a bed."

"Yes," she said. "That's what I'm asking."

"Then my answer is yes."

She drove home quickly, anticipation thrumming through her body. Gideon didn't touch her as they walked up the steps and into the house. When the door was closed, he pulled her back against his chest. Arms circling her waist, he nibbled at her neck. "You're awfully tense," he murmured. "Are you sure you want me here?"

"I'm sure," she whispered. "I'm just a little nervous." Foolish, after what they'd just done in the car. But it felt like a huge step for Gideon to stay the night.

He let her go and took her hand. "Then why don't you show me your bedroom and we'll see what we can do about those nerves."

HIS SKIN WAS cooling, but Gideon didn't want to move. Couldn't bear to move. Tiny aftershocks of the most intense climax he'd ever experienced were still zinging through him. He wanted to stay just like he was, joined to Zoe. And that was scary.

He wasn't ready to be accountable to someone else. To be responsible for someone else.

He never had been. If he was, he would have protected his brother from his father. He would have seen what kind of monster his father had become.

Zoe moved against him, and he pushed his father out of his mind. He didn't want to think about him tonight.

Zoe's arms were wrapped tightly around him, and

she'd curled one of her legs around his thigh. Almost as if she was a part of him.

He rolled to his back, pulling her with him so she was lying on top of him. "That was amazing," he murmured into her neck. He stroked her back, lingered at her rear. "*You're* amazing."

She propped herself on her elbows and touched his mouth. "Thank you, Gideon," she said.

"For what?"

"For taking care of my nerves." She grinned. "I'm thinking I should get nervous more often."

He pulled her close and felt her heart beating against his. "Anytime, sweetheart."

"Necking at the park was fun, but it was kind of like eating candy when you're really hungry," she said drowsily. "It takes the edge off, but doesn't fill you up."

"And now?"

"Now it feels like I just ate a seven-course dinner," she said. "Completely satisfied."

"Completely?" He bit her neck gently. When she shuddered, he rolled over and slid her beneath him. "We haven't had dessert yet."

ZOE WAS SOUND ASLEEP, sprawled in the moonlight that pooled on the bed, one hand extended toward him. He'd been asleep, too, but something had awakened him.

He held his breath, listening. There it was again. A creaking noise. Coming from the back of the house.

Slipping out of bed, he silently pulled on his jeans, then headed for the kitchen. A pair of windows looking onto the backyard were half-covered with curtains. Moonlight poured through and spilled onto the table.

One curtain lifted gently, as if an air current had drifted through the room.

There was no intruder in the house. But he hadn't imagined that sound.

As he walked toward the windows, several boards creaked beneath his feet. Damn it!

Outside, something hit the ground with a thud and footsteps retreated. Yanking back the curtain, he stared into the darkness.

The porch at the rear of the house extended about five feet on either side of the back door. A barbecue grill hunched in the shadows in front of him, and two patio chairs gleamed in the moonlight.

A man was running toward the garage.

After fumbling with the lock, he yanked open the back door and tripped over something hard on the porch. Catching himself on the railing, he leaped down the stairs and ran toward where the man had disappeared. As he reached the garage, he heard the rumble of a car engine starting on the street behind Zoe's house.

The intruder would be gone before he could reach him. And he didn't want to leave Zoe alone.

At the top of the steps, he saw a rectangular shape off to the side. A brick with a note wrapped around it. He was crouched down, trying to read what was written on the paper without touching it, when Zoe came to the door. She wore a robe and had her arms wrapped around her waist.

"What's going on, Gideon?"

"I heard a noise and came to check it out. I saw someone running away."

"And you ran after him?" she said sharply. "What were you thinking?"

"You were perfectly safe," he said, rising to his feet. "I was never out of sight of the back door."

"I didn't mean I was scared," she said, throwing the light switch on. "I meant you could have been hurt." She noticed the brick at his feet. "What's that?"

"It was on the porch," he said. "It says, 'Mind your own business, bitch.'"

"Nice," she said, sounding disgusted. "What fool left that here?"

"Zoe, he was probably getting ready to throw that through your window," he said, shocked that she could be so cavalier about it.

"It wouldn't be the first time," she said, nudging the brick away from the door with her toe. "Come back into the house, Gideon. We'll deal with it in the morning."

"We're phoning the police right now," he said. "They might be able to catch the guy who was going to throw it."

"He's probably home by now," she said impatiently. "Spruce Lake is a small town."

"We should still call 9-1-1."

"I'll call the police in the morning," she repeated. "There's nothing anyone can do tonight."

"Go back to bed," he said. "I'll make sure nothing else has been disturbed."

ZOE WOKE UP in a beam of sunlight. It warmed her and she stretched, enjoying the heat on her bare skin.

Memories of the night before crowded into her mind, and she smiled as she turned and reached for Gideon. Her hand found only cold sheets. His head had left an indentation in the pillow, but it, too, was cold.

She reached for the quilt and pulled it tightly around

her as she stared at the empty bed. Had he left without waking her up? Without saying goodbye?

Even after the brick incident in the early-morning hours?

Maybe he'd been angry because she didn't call the police right away.

They'd had sex last night. Several times. It had been fabulous, but now it was morning and he was gone. Was she supposed to go back to her regularly scheduled life as if nothing unusual or different had happened? Pretend that she was fine waking up alone after a night of love-making? Is that what adults did—enjoyed the moment and moved on?

She picked up the pillow Gideon had used and threw it against the wall, then stripped the sheets from the bed. The scent of him, of their lovemaking, permeated everything. She stuffed the linens into her laundry hamper and shrugged into her robe, yanking the belt into a knot.

It was just as well he was gone, she told herself. If he had stayed, she might have blurted out something she didn't mean. Something she'd regret later. This was better. She'd have time to steady herself, time to get her emotions under control. Taking a deep breath, she headed for the kitchen to start the coffee. She was going to need lots of it today.

Gideon stood at one of the kitchen windows, doing something with a screwdriver. He glanced over his shoulder. "Good morning," he said.

"I—I thought you'd left," she stammered.

"Nope. You think I'd leave without making sure you were safe?" He turned to the window and resumed his handyman act.

"What are you doing, Gideon?"

"I'm replacing your window locks. They were way too loose. A kid could jimmy them open."

"What?" She hurried over to the window. Her graceful old brass window latch had disappeared, replaced by a large, ugly silver one, with a slot in it for a key. "Where did you get that?"

"The hardware store," he said. "They open early in the morning."

He'd already replaced the latch on the other kitchen window. And the lock on her back door was new, too. Her stomach twisted as she stared at it. "Don't you think you should have asked me before you did this?" she said, trying to stifle her annoyance. He was trying to be helpful. He thought he was doing something nice for her.

"I wanted to get it finished before you had to leave for the shelter," he said. "So your house would be secure while you're gone."

"No one's going to break in during the day."

"You sure about that?"

"Where's that brick with the note?" she asked.

"The police took it. They're going to check the note for fingerprints."

"You called the police while I was still in bed?" she said slowly, irritation turning to anger.

"You didn't get much sleep last night," he said. "I didn't want to disturb you."

"Gideon, stop with the windows," she said sharply. "We need to talk."

"What's wrong?" he said, turning around.

She took a deep breath. "I know you mean well, but don't you think you've gone a little overboard? Changing my locks, calling the police?" One of the old latches lay on the kitchen table, a deep gouge in the brass. "Taking out my antique window hardware that I searched for months to find?"

"They were loose. They made it easy to break into the house," he said as if puzzled that she was upset.

"I don't care. They were mine. They're what I wanted on my windows. You had no right removing them without asking me first."

He set the screwdriver carefully on the table. "I just wanted to make sure you were protected."

She didn't feel protected. She felt crowded into a corner. Smothered.

Controlled.

"You're trying to run my life. Acting as if I'm not smart enough to look after myself." She picked up the old latch and rubbed at the scratch in the metal. "I think you should leave, Gideon," she said.

He picked up her tools and replaced them carefully in the kitchen drawer where he'd found them. "That was the last window. The new keys for the door are on the table."

She watched him walk down the street until he was out of sight. Then, glancing at the bulky latches on her living room windows, she leaned against the door.

So much for the happily ever after she'd been fantasizing about when she woke up this morning. Let down your guard with a man, allow him into your bed, and the next thing you know, he thinks he's in charge of you.

That was what she got for thinking the fantasy was real. No one stumbles out of bed in the morning and decides they're in love.

Great sex didn't make you fall in love.

No. You have great sex because you've fallen in love.

She couldn't be in love with Gideon. He was just like his brother, thinking he owned her.

She would never be anyone's property again.

Not even Gideon's.

CHAPTER EIGHTEEN

"SEE WHAT YOU can do, Helen. Get a restraining order. He's frightening his wife and he's beginning to irritate me."

"I'll get on it, Zo."

Zoe set the phone down and shoved a hand through her hair as she tossed Marilu Halvorsen's file onto the cluttered surface of her desk, pulling two pink message slips from beneath it. Marilu's husband, Jesse, just wouldn't take no for an answer. He'd been hounding her ever since Jamie Evans brought Marilu and their daughter to the shelter.

He'd started out trying to sweet-talk Zoe. Then he'd spoken to her as if she was a slow child, telling her that his wife and baby needed him.

Now he was threatening her. In her current mood, a confrontation sounded like a good idea, but she was smarter than that. Or she should be.

Her hand tightened on the phone. Could he be the person who'd left the brick on her porch last night?

She definitely needed to call the police. Maybe by now they'd found fingerprints on the note.

It was a good thing the police were already involved, she admitted reluctantly. Even though she was still angry at the way Gideon had done it.

Before she could dial, the phone rang again. She

snatched it up and said, "Mr. Halvorsen, I told you not to call here anymore. Your wife doesn't want to talk to you."

"Uh, hi, Zo," said her sister Bree.

"Bree. Sorry." Zoe rubbed her gritty eyes. "I thought you were someone else."

"Someone hassling you?"

"Yes, but I should have looked at the caller ID." Her lack of sleep the night before and the emotions roiling inside her all day made her feel as if she were in a fog. "What's up?"

"I heard more at school today," Bree said softly. "About Barb."

"Hold on." Zoe closed the door to her office. "What did you hear?"

"A bunch of teachers are going out to dinner tonight, and then bowling. They asked me if I wanted to go."

"That's great, Bree. It sounds like fun. Do you need someone to stay with Charlie?"

"Thanks, but Fiona's going to be here, anyway. I think they're going to get a pizza." Bree sounded surprised that Zoe would offer, and it was a tiny stab to Zoe's heart. She wished she'd spent more time with her nephew. "You can join them, though. Charlie would love it."

"Maybe I will," Zoe said, her heart lightening. "Thanks. But what does Barb have to do with it?"

"The teachers asked her to come bowling, too. But she said she was busy tonight. I thought she was still at the shelter."

"She is," Zoe said, glancing at the schedule on the whiteboard hanging on the wall. There was a self-defense workshop that evening. "We've got a program tonight. That's probably what she was talking about."

"Okay." Bree sounded relieved. "I'm glad there's a logical explanation."

"Thanks for the call, though. I appreciate it."

"No problem, Zo. That shelter helps a lot of women and kids. I don't want anyone taking advantage of you."

Zoe swallowed the sudden lump in her throat. "Thanks, Bree. That means a lot."

"Yeah, you found the perfect way to use that bossy gene of yours," Bree said lightly.

"I guess I did," Zoe said with a laugh. "Have fun tonight."

Surprised and warmed by Bree's words, Zoe grabbed her mug and headed for the coffee urn in the living room. Barb had been in there earlier.

She still was, writing in a journal. Two toddlers played on the floor while their mothers sat on a couch, talking in low voices.

"How are you doing, Barb?" Zoe asked, dropping into a chair next to her, far enough away from the other women to give them privacy.

"I'm fine, Zoe." Barb smiled. "Thanks for asking."

"How is your case going? Is your attorney prepping you to testify?"

Barb's smile faltered and she glanced away. "I've talked to her on the phone a few times. She has a hard time getting here from Green Bay."

"It's a bit of a drive," Zoe agreed. She wanted to ask Barb, again, why she hadn't hired an attorney from Spruce Lake, but this wasn't the time. "A woman from the martial arts studio is coming in to teach a self-defense class tonight. Will you be there?"

Barb clicked her pen several times. "I don't think so," she said. "I'm still a little sore."

"You could just listen and watch. You'd learn a lot that way."

"I was kind of hoping to take a long bath while everyone else is at the presentation, then go to bed early."

"It's up to you, Barb," Zoe said easily. "You know we don't force you to do anything here but group sessions."

"Thanks, Zoe."

Zoe got a cup of coffee she didn't need. Was Bree right? Was Barb going to leave the shelter to meet a lover?

ZOE SAT IN HER CAR a few hours later, grateful the shelter was on a corner lot. It made it so much easier to spy on people. She leaned forward to wipe a trace of condensation from the windshield. It was too bad such surveillance was necessary.

She'd parked on the street that ran along the side of the shelter, positioned so she could see anyone leaving from either the front or the back door. The window was open a crack to help keep the windows clear, and she was freezing. It was the coldest night of April, and she'd been here for more than an hour. There had been no sign of Barb or anyone else leaving the building.

She felt like a traitor for not trusting Barb. There was probably a perfectly logical explanation, Zoe told herself. Maybe Barb hadn't wanted to get together with her fellow teachers and was doing exactly what she'd said—taking a bath and going to bed.

Her phone rang and she checked the screen, biting her lip when she saw his name. "Hello, Gideon."

"Hi, Zoe. What are you up to?" He sounded cautious, as if he wasn't sure of his reception.

"I'm still at the shelter. I'm…checking on something."

"How about dinner? I think we need to talk."

She'd intended to say the same thing the next time she saw him, but he'd beaten her to the punch. "I agree, but I'm not sure when I'll be finished." There was silence at the other end of the phone. Did he think she was fabricating excuses to avoid him? "I'm not blowing you off, Gideon," she said. "I just have a situation here and I'm not sure when I can get away."

"What kind of situation?" he asked sharply.

"Nothing bad or dangerous," she assured him. "Just some issues that have come up with a resident. I'm hoping they can be resolved quickly."

"Okay." He hesitated. "Do you want to give me a call when you're finished?"

"It might be late."

"I don't care," he said. She could hear his fingers tapping on a hard surface. "I'd like to see you, Zoe."

Her pulse quickened. "I'd like to see you, too." She still wanted him, in spite of what had happened that morning.

"Call me." He hung up without waiting for her to reply.

Snapping her phone closed, she stared toward the shelter, not really seeing it. Instead, she saw Gideon's face, taut with passion the night before. Kissing her. Making love with her.

Standing in the kitchen with a screwdriver, replacing the hardware on her windows and doors.

Damn it, why had he gone caveman on her? She'd thought he was different, that he had enough self-confidence that he didn't have to dominate a woman. Had her judgment about a man failed her again?

She planned on finding out tonight.

ZOE WAS GETTING ready to admit that Barb wasn't going anywhere when a car rolled to a stop at the shelter's front door and sat there for a few minutes. Then it turned the corner and stopped at the curb several houses down. The driver kept the car running—she could see exhaust streaming out of the tailpipe.

Zoe wiped the windshield again with her sleeve and squinted, trying to read the license plate. But half a block separated the two cars, and she couldn't make it out. It was a sedan, nondescript and ordinary. She thought it was dark green.

Was the driver waiting for someone from the shelter? Barb, maybe? She turned on her engine, rolling slowly down the street, trying to see the plate. But it was spattered with mud, and she could only make out two of the letters and one number.

Maybe it wasn't Barb's lover, she thought uneasily. Maybe it was someone else. Someone like Jesse Halvorsen, who had threatened her earlier.

She reached for her purse and fumbled for her cell phone, but it was lost in the jumble of her belongings. She held the purse wide open as she dug through her wallet, makeup pouch and papers. She'd call the police and ask them to do a drive-by and check the guy out.

Out of the corner of her eye she saw a man get out of the car and trot toward her. Dropping her purse, she reached into the backseat for the baseball bat she kept on the floor. A man she didn't recognize put his hands on her side window and peered into the car.

"Who are you?" he asked. "What are you doing here?"

Zoe shifted the bat in her hands, making sure the man could see it. "Who are *you?* And what are *you* doing here?"

He leaned closer, as if trying to see who she was. "None of your damn business. Are you spying on me?"

"That depends on why you're here."

He glanced at the shelter, then slapped her door. "The hell with this," he muttered, running to his car and climbing in. The gears ground, then he roared away from the curb.

She needed to know who he was. They didn't advertise the shelter's location, but it wouldn't be too difficult to find if someone was determined enough.

Or had a grudge.

Dropping the bat onto the seat next to her, she pulled out and followed him. She drove too fast down the side street, watching the taillights a couple of blocks ahead of her. He turned right, and she caught up just in time to see him pull onto Main Street.

The four stoplights downtown stayed green long enough for him to speed through them. As he accelerated through the residential area on the outskirts of town, Zoe drove faster. She ran two yellow lights, but the next one was red, and she reluctantly came to a stop. By the time it turned green, she'd lost him.

Damn it. She pulled to the side of the road, hoping she'd spot him again, knowing it was hopeless. At least she had part of his license plate number.

Finally she turned around and headed back through town to the shelter. She checked with Sharon, the housemother, but nothing unusual had happened that evening. As far as Sharon knew, no one had left the house.

As she was getting back in her car, her phone rang. Gideon. "Hi," she said. "I'm just finishing up here. I'll be home in a few minutes."

There was a pause at the other end of the line. "I just came from the shelter," he finally said. "They told me you left a couple of hours ago."

"It's complicated," she answered. "As far as they know, I did."

"What's going on, Zoe?" His voice sharpened. "Are you all right?"

"I'm fine. If you want to come to the house, I'll tell you about it."

"I'll meet you there."

Edgy anticipation hummed through her as she started her car. In spite of the uncomfortable way they'd parted, in spite of her doubts about her own judgment, she still wanted to see Gideon.

Her heart beat hard against her ribs as she drove to meet him.

GIDEON SAT on Zoe's porch swing, the white bag holding the dinner he'd bought for her at the Pasta Bowl on the seat beside him. It had long since gotten cold.

He saw her headlights approaching and hurried down the porch stairs. Her car had barely stopped when he opened the door. "Zoe. Are you okay?"

"I'm fine," she said, tilting her head. "Why would you think I wasn't?"

"You sounded pretty mysterious on the phone."

"Just a long day." She sighed.

"I'll get your briefcase," he said, reaching into the car.

Instead of the briefcase, he found a wooden baseball bat propped against the passenger seat. "Were you playing ball today?" he asked her.

"No, that's Louie." She dropped it on the floor behind the front seats. "Short for Louisville Slugger. I keep him in the car in case I run into an angry husband."

Fear made him grab her. "What were you doing, Zoe?"

She glanced at his hand on her arm. "I'll tell you

about it inside," she said, gently detaching herself from his grip. "I'm freezing."

While she unlocked the door, he picked up the white bag from the swing. "What's that?" she said as she stepped inside and turned on the lights.

"I figured you'd probably missed dinner," he said. "It's spinach lasagna from the Pasta Bowl."

"You remembered what I ordered when we went there," she said, warmth filling her eyes. "Thank you, Gideon." She kissed him on the cheek, stepping away before he could pull her closer.

He was no expert at relationships, but theirs had clearly cooled since the previous night. Was she embarrassed because she'd gotten angry that morning?

"I'll heat it up if you want to put something warmer on," he said.

"Thanks. I'll be right out."

She went into her bedroom and closed the door. Another clue. There was definitely something wrong.

As the lasagna heated, he checked the windows and the back door. Nothing looked like it had been disturbed. He was inspecting the living room windows when she reappeared, wearing jeans and a sweater.

"I'm glad you…"

"What was going on…"

They spoke at the same time, then stopped, awkwardly. "You first," Zoe finally said, sitting on the couch.

Her hand was still cold when he touched it, and he rubbed it between his. "You were going to tell me what was going on at the shelter."

She sighed and tucked her feet beneath her, but she left her hand in his. That had to be a good sign. "Someone told me one of the women at Safe Harbor might be using us as a cover for having an affair," she said. "I was told she might be sneaking out tonight to meet her lover, so I sat in my car to see what happened."

"No wonder you're cold," he said.

"Yeah, I was out there for more than an hour. That's where I was when you called the first time."

"So what happened?"

As she told him about the vehicle she'd spotted and the man who'd come up to her car, he tensed. Instinctively he tightened his hold on her hand.

"Then he drove off," she said. "So I followed him. But I was caught by a stoplight and lost him. I never saw more than those three digits from his license plate."

"You followed him?" He stared at her, appalled. "Zoe, what were you thinking?"

"I needed to know who he was. To know who had found the shelter. Maybe it was the guy waiting for his lover, but what if it was a man whose wife was in there? That would have been dangerous."

She sounded as if following a possibly aggressive man was a reasonable thing to do. "Why didn't you call the police?"

"He would have been long gone by the time they got to the shelter."

Gideon twisted to face her. "My God, Zoe! What's wrong with you?"

CHAPTER NINETEEN

"WHAT DID YOU SAY?" She drew back her hand and shifted to the end of the couch. Away from him.

"I asked what's wrong with you? Why you thought it was a good idea to follow some pissed-off guy who had already confronted you once."

"I wanted to get his license plate number." She frowned. "I was perfectly safe."

"That's why you had a baseball bat on the seat next to you?"

"I've had Louie in my car since I opened the shelter," she said evenly. "This is a small town, and people know who I am. I have no intention of being afraid all the time. I had enough of that when I was married."

Why couldn't Zoe see that what she'd done was dangerous? That she'd put herself at risk?

He jumped to his feet. "Look, Zoe, I get it. You can take care of yourself. You're a smart, capable woman. But confronting an angry man by yourself is a damn stupid thing to do."

She flinched as if he'd hit her. "Don't call me stupid, Gideon." She swallowed, twice, and wrapped her arms around herself. "And I didn't confront him. I didn't get out of the car. I never put myself in danger."

"What did you hope to accomplish?"

"I wanted to find out if Barb was using us."

"Barb? Was this about Barb Johnson?"

She paled. "Forget I said that, Gideon."

"I don't give a damn about Barb Johnson. And I can't believe we're having this conversation after what happened last night," Gideon said, locking his hands behind his head so he didn't try to shake some sense into her. Watching her intruder running through the yard had terrified him.

"Yes," she said, drawing herself up. "Let's talk about last night. And this morning."

"What about this morning?" He'd done a good thing for her. He'd made her house more secure. He'd protected her. That was what a man was supposed to do for the woman he lo... For someone he cared about.

"Why did you go out and get those window latches so early? Couldn't you have waited to talk to me about them first?"

"They needed to be replaced. I assumed you'd agree with me." He watched her uneasily.

"This is my house, Gideon," she said, her voice low. She got to her feet. "It's for me to decide what to do about the windows and the door. Just like waiting outside the shelter and following that car was my choice. Derrick always told me what to do. He made all the decisions. He tried to take away my power. I swore I would never let that happen again."

"Are you saying I'm like Derrick?" he asked, incredulous.

"I know you'd never hurt me. I'm not afraid of you, if that's what you're asking. But men overpower women in more subtle ways than with their fists. You're trying to control me. To tell me what to do and how to act." She scraped her hair off her forehead, and he saw her hand shaking. Badly. "Do you understand what I'm saying?"

He thought of the brother he couldn't protect and the guilt he'd lived with for the past six years. Now Zoe was telling him he couldn't keep her safe, either, and he lost his temper.

"Fine," he said, his voice rising. "Put the old window latches back on. Use the old door locks that a ten-year-old could break open. Leave yourself vulnerable to every crazy who decides you're the enemy. Just don't expect me to stick around to watch it happen. I'm not going to wait for another person I lo…care about to get hurt. Or killed."

He yanked the door open and stormed out, slamming it behind him. He was almost at the street when he saw Zoe's face in his mind. Her mouth had been trembling, and her face was paper white. As he'd yelled, she'd backed against the wall.

Surely she hadn't gotten that upset about an argument. He'd never seen her walk away from a fight. There was something else going on.

Turning around, he ran back up the stairs and tried to open the door. But it was locked. He peered through the window, but didn't see her. Maybe she'd gone into the kitchen to eat the lasagna.

He heard a whimper, the kind of sound an animal in pain would make. Then he spotted her.

She was curled up on the floor in a corner of the living room, her knees drawn up to her head. Her arms were wrapped around her legs like she was trying to hold herself together. Her shoulders shook with the force of her sobs.

"Zoe!" he shouted through the window. "What's wrong?"

She didn't look at him. He wasn't sure she even heard him.

He ran back to the door and tried to open it. But the new locks he'd installed worked as advertised. It was shut tight.

"Zoe!" he screamed, pounding on the wood. "Open the door."

God! What should he do? He couldn't get to her, couldn't help her.

Her sisters. She needed her sisters.

Sprinting to his car, he dove in and had it moving before he buckled his seat belt. Zoe had pointed out her father's house once, and that was where her sisters were staying. He drove faster and hoped they were home.

"ZOE? ZOE, I SEE YOU in there." The doorknob rattled. "Open up."

Bree's voice. What was she doing here? Zoe lifted her head and wiped away the tears. Was something wrong with Charlie? Or Fiona?

She struggled to her feet and stumbled out to the hallway. It took too long to open the unfamiliar locks, but finally she managed it. Bree stepped inside, turned and nodded, then closed the door.

"What's wrong?" Zoe said, wiping her face with the backs of her hands. "Is it Charlie?" She grabbed her sister's arm. "His heart?"

"Charlie is fine," Bree said, wrapping her arms around Zoe and holding her tightly. "It's okay, Zoe."

"What?" It was as if something had short-circuited in her brain. "What are you talking about?"

"Gideon got me. He said you needed me." She rocked Zoe back and forth. "You want to tell me what happened?"

What had happened? "It was awful. Gideon and I

were having a fight," Zoe whispered. "He yelled at me and said I was stupid." She held more tightly to Bree. "All I could see was Derrick. He called me that all the time. Usually right before he hit me."

Bree frowned. "Gideon called you stupid? Really? He was worried sick about you."

"He was mad about something I did." She stepped away from the comfort of her sister. "When he started shouting at me, my memories of Derrick mixed together with Gideon in my head. Whenever Gideon spoke, it was as if Derrick was in my house, screaming at me."

She was so cold. Ice had penetrated her chest, freezing her lungs. And her heart.

"You had a flashback," Bree said gently. "I'm no shrink, but even I know that much." She curled her arm around Zoe and steered her to the couch. "Sit down and talk about it if you want. Or not. Fiona's with Charlie. I can stay as long as you like."

Zoe took a deep, shaky breath. "It started last night," she said. "This morning, really."

She told her sister about the intruder and about the brick. How she'd woken up alone and found Gideon in the kitchen. "He changed the window latches, Bree. And the locks on the doors. Without even asking me."

"That bastard," she said lightly. "What was he thinking, trying to keep you safe?"

"He should have asked me first," Zoe said.

"Yeah, he should have. I'd have torn him a new one, too. But I'm guessing he went into protective mode and didn't think. That I-must-protect-the-homestead-and-the-womenfolk mind-set is genetically programmed in men."

"Not all of them," Zoe said.

"No." Bree's arm tightened around her shoulders.

"Only the good ones. Look, Zo, he overstepped, no question about that. But it sounds like he did it because he cares about you." She rubbed Zoe's back. "He was pretty upset when he came to get me."

"Are you taking his side?"

"Of course not." Bree scowled. "He's a Tate. As far as I'm concerned, he's on probation. And he's going to stay there for a while. What he did was wrong, Zo, but he did it for the right reasons."

"I swore I would never let anyone control me again," Zoe said, pulling the afghan around her. "It felt as if he was telling me what to do."

"He was," Bree said. "If you keep him, he's going to need some training. But I'm guessing he's educable."

Zoe chuckled weakly. "How can you make me laugh when I'm feeling so bad?"

"It's a gift," Bree said.

Zoe's smile faded. "It is, Bree. You always cheered us up. It was the only thing that helped when Dad was ranting and raving. You even made *him* laugh sometimes." Zoe clung to her hand. "Thanks."

Bree held her close. "My pleasure, Zo." She eased away. "Are you okay now?"

"Yes," Zoe said, taking a deep, shuddering breath. "I'm okay."

"He's waiting on the porch," Bree said. "He'd like to make sure you're all right."

"I can't talk to him tonight," Zoe said, humiliation curling in her stomach.

"Are you sure?"

"I don't know what to say to him. I haven't dated anyone since Derrick. Now, I meet a man I care about, and I act like a crazy person when we have a fight."

"So now he knows you're not perfect." Bree shrugged. "Apparently that's not one of his requirements in a woman." She hugged Zoe once more, then stood up. "I'm going home. Do you want me to let him in or tell him to go away?"

"I don't know," Zoe said.

"He's not going anywhere until he knows you're all right," Bree said. "So unless you want him sleeping on your front porch, you'd better see him." She waggled her eyebrows at Zoe. "At least I'm giving you a choice. If Fiona had come over, she'd have stared you down until you did whatever she wanted you to do."

"I take back every nice thing I just said about you," Zoe muttered.

"Yeah, yeah. I love you, too." Bree kissed her cheek. "I'll talk to you tomorrow, okay?"

Zoe took a deep breath. "Okay."

Moments later Gideon stepped into the house and closed the door, then leaned against it. "Are you all right?"

"You mean for a crazy woman?"

"You scared the hell out of me."

"I scared myself."

"What was that all about?" he said, still at the door.

"You can come in and sit down," she said with a sigh. "I'm not going to lose it again."

He sank warily onto the couch. Was he waiting for her to go off again?

"I had a flashback," she said quietly. "Calling me stupid sparked it. Derrick said that all the time. It was like…" She bit her lip, hating that she was comparing him to his brother. But she wanted him to understand.

"Is it because Derrick was my brother? Is that why it happened?"

"No. Maybe. I don't know. That's probably part of it, but it was the whole situation—you trying to tell me what to do, not listening to what I was saying, telling me I was stupid."

He studied her without saying anything. She knew how she looked—her eyes red and swollen, her face tearstained, her hair a mess. But she wasn't going to apologize for losing it. Her history was part of who she was. And Gideon had been wrong.

"You don't want anyone to take care of you, is that it?" he said. "You want to prove you can look after yourself."

"I don't want anyone to ride roughshod over me and not listen to what I have to say," she retorted. "I don't want to be protected by being smothered."

"And that's what I was doing? Smothering you?"

"You didn't give me a choice about the doors and windows," she said. "*You* decided what I needed. I have to have choices, Gideon."

He nodded slowly. "I have choices, too, Zoe. I've blamed myself for six years because I wasn't able to protect Derrick. Because I hadn't been closer to him. I don't ever want to feel that way again. I don't know if I can step aside and let you put yourself at risk."

"You think your guilt gives you the right to tell me what to do? If so, that's pretty ironic, isn't it? Because I'm the reason you've been carrying that guilt. I'm the one you didn't protect him against." Gideon was pulling away from her, and she wasn't sure how to stop it. How to repair the rift that had cracked open between them. A rift that was widening.

"I thought so for a long time. Now I know that it's my father's fault."

"But I played a role." She moved to the window. "I

thought we could get past what happened to Derrick. It was fine when it was all fun and games. This is the first real disagreement we've had, and everything fell apart. I'm guessing that doesn't bode well for the future."

"Do you want a future with me, Zoe?"

Yes. "Does it matter? It doesn't sound as if you want to be with me, not on my terms."

"You're asking me to be someone I'm not."

"No, I'm asking you to look at this through my eyes," she said quietly. "And it doesn't seem as though you can."

"I'm trying. But I don't agree with you. And I won't pretend that I do."

She nodded, trying to hold herself together. "All right, Gideon. If I decide I want to be wrapped in cotton wool and protected from the world, I'll let you know. If you decide you can let me be myself, you can let *me* know. Until then, it's probably better if we don't see each other."

The words made her heart break, but she couldn't think what else to do. She wasn't about to choose between Gideon and her hard-won self-confidence and independence. It had taken her too long, and too much anguish, to get to here.

"Goodbye, Zoe," he said. He looked as if he was about to say something else, then he turned and walked out the door.

CHAPTER TWENTY

GIDEON SAT next to Dave in the small conference room he'd borrowed at a local attorney's office and watched Dave adjust his tie for the fifth or sixth time. Why was Dave so nervous? He'd said he wanted a chance to confront Barb, and that was what he was getting.

Gideon was the one who should be nervous. Zoe was going to feel as if he'd ambushed her, and she wasn't going to be happy about it.

Whatever the outcome, this little get-together would probably draw a final line through their already ruptured relationship.

He'd talked to her on the phone since the night she'd told him to leave, but only about business. No matter how much he wanted her, how much he ached for her, she was asking too much of him. Just as she couldn't change for him, he couldn't change for her.

Heels tapped in the hallway. Two sets. Gideon took a deep breath. Zoe had brought Barb. They were going to be finished with this case today, one way or another. Then maybe he could start forgetting her.

Fat chance of that.

Zoe walked into the conference room in a killer red outfit, and Gideon nodded at her. She knew how to play the game. First rule was wear the power suit.

Then she spotted Dave and stopped. "You didn't tell me he was going to be here."

"You didn't ask." Barb stood frozen in the doorway, a mixture of apprehension and shame on her face. "Come in and have a seat, Barb. We need to discuss some things."

"Barb doesn't want to talk to Dave," Zoe said sharply. "She'll do her talking at the trial."

"I think we can get this straightened out today," Gideon said, his voice calm. "You don't want this hanging over your head any more than Dave does, do you, Barb?"

"No," she said reluctantly. "I guess not."

"Right. Then have a seat."

Zoe guided Barb to the other side of the table, keeping her as far away from Dave as possible. Zoe sat down across from Gideon, her mouth a tight line. "You better have a good reason for this," she said.

"I do." He nodded at Dave. "My client doesn't know why we're here, either. But I received some information that I believe has a bearing on this case."

Zoe gasped. "Don't you dare, Gideon," she said in a low voice.

Ignoring her, he said, "Barb, is it true that you're having an affair and concocted the allegations against my client in an attempt to hide the relationship?"

"What?" Barb's face went white. Her panicked gaze flicked between Gideon and Dave. "Who told you that?"

"Does it matter?"

"Of course it matters." She pulled herself together, and Gideon admired her nerve. "That's exactly the kind of story Dave would make up," she said.

It was a nice recovery, but Barb had always been

sharp-witted. "I didn't hear it from Dave," Gideon said. Dave, shocked, was staring at Barb. "Is it true?"

"Of course not," she said quickly. Too quickly.

"Let's go, Barb," Zoe said, standing up. She put her hand on Barb's shoulder. "You don't have to talk to him."

"No, you don't," Gideon said, ignoring Zoe and focusing on Barb. "You're not under oath. I can't force you to answer. But what's going to happen at Dave's trial?" he asked softly. "Then you *will* be under oath. I have plenty of time to find your lover and subpoena him. At the trial, you'll both be compelled to testify."

"Can he do that?" Barb asked Zoe, fear in her eyes.

"Yes, he can make you testify at a trial. And you'd have to tell the truth." Zoe sank slowly back into her chair. "Is he right, Barb? Did you make up the story about Dave hitting you to conceal an affair?"

Tears rolled down the woman's face, staining the white silk of her blouse. She knotted her hands together in her lap and nodded. "Yes."

Zoe leaned closer. "You lied to me."

"Yes," Barb whispered.

"Did Dave ever hit you?" Zoe demanded.

"I wish he had." Barb jerked her head up and glared at Dave. "It would have been better than what he did. I'd rather he punched me and got it over with!" Barb cried. "He criticizes me constantly and tells me I'm silly and fat. He tells me I can't do anything right. No matter what happens, I'm always wrong. He was beating me down, and I couldn't take it anymore."

"So you got involved with someone else?" Zoe said. "How was that supposed to help?"

"I hadn't had sex in over a year," Barb said, fresh

tears streaming down her face. "He told me no one would want to go to bed with a cow like me."

"So you went out and proved him wrong," Gideon said quietly.

"I didn't intend to have an affair. It just…happened." Barb cupped her face in her hands and sobbed, rocking back and forth. Zoe put an arm around her.

Gideon glanced at Dave, trying to hide his distaste. No wonder Dave and Derrick had been friends. "Do you want to say something?"

"She's exaggerating," he muttered. "It wasn't that bad."

"So Barb is telling the truth?" Gideon asked.

"I guess I've been pretty mean to her."

"You guess? Have you said those things or not?"

Dave pushed his glass of water across the table from one hand to the other. "I say things I don't mean when I get angry," he said.

"I'll take that as a yes," Gideon said.

On the other side of the table, Zoe's eyes were filled with contempt. For him or for Dave? "What do you think we should do here, Ms. McInnes?"

"I don't think much of either Dave or Barb right now," she said. "I'm tempted to say they deserve each other. But that wouldn't solve anyone's problems."

Dave ignored Zoe as he fiddled with a pen now, and Gideon wished he could simply walk away. Instead, he elbowed Dave. "Pay attention," he said sharply.

As Dave looked up at her, Zoe said, "Emotional abuse is just as damaging as physical abuse and the scars last a lot longer, Dave. A man who would say those things to his wife is despicable. I can't force you, but you need help. I suggest you find a therapist and get started."

At least Dave had the grace to look ashamed of himself. Gideon thought he'd known this man, known what kind of person he was. He hadn't known Dave at all.

"Are you the one who filed the zoning complaint to the city council?" Zoe asked.

After a long moment, Dave nodded.

"I expect you to make it go away," Zoe said. "Or I'll tell the council who is responsible. And why. Do you understand me, Dave?"

"Yeah," he finally said. "I'll take care of it."

"And, you, Barb." Zoe didn't raise her voice, but Gideon wouldn't want to be on the receiving end of the fury in her eyes. "Dave wasn't hitting you, but he *was* mistreating you. You could have used our shelter if you needed some time away from him. You didn't have to lie. Do you understand what you've done?"

Barb shrugged. "I'm in trouble. I get it."

"I know it's a stretch, Barb, but try to think of more than just yourself," Zoe said. "You put every one of us at Safe Harbor in danger when you gave your lover our location. You damaged our mission, as well. Every time a woman fabricates abuse, she hurts the credibility of women everywhere. You made it harder for all the women who *are* being beaten. And you made it easier for the people who don't want to believe it."

"I didn't think," Barb said, her head bowed. "I was desperate to get away."

"You could have just left him," Zoe said, her voice softening. "People get divorced all the time."

"I... I'm sorry," Barb whispered.

Nobody said anything for a long moment. Gideon tried to catch Zoe's eye, but she wouldn't look at him. She was staring at Barb.

"You betrayed me, Barb," she finally said, and her

voice was laced with pain. "I believed you without question, and you lied to me." She leaned closer to the other woman. "Every time someone comes to Safe Harbor now, I'm going to look at her a little differently. Trust her a little less. Wonder if she's telling me the truth."

She took Barb's hand. "Do you know what it does to an abused woman when she thinks no one believes her? It makes her shrivel up inside, squashes the tiny bit of hope that she can get through it. It makes her feel more helpless, more powerless. More completely alone."

Zoe was talking about herself, Gideon realized. About what she'd experienced when she was married to his brother. No wonder she guarded her independence so fiercely.

No wonder control was so important to her.

"I didn't mean to hurt anyone," Barb murmured. "I just didn't know what else to do."

"You could have been honest with me," Zoe said. "I would have helped you.

"You're going to have to repay the shelter for the time you spent there," Zoe finally said to Barb. "You understand why, don't you?"

"Yes," Barb said. "I'll pay you back."

"And you'll go to therapy?"

Barb nodded.

Zoe turned her attention to Dave. "Whether you want to save your marriage or not is up to both of you. If you want to try, I'll give you the names of some good couples counselors."

"Fine," Dave muttered. "Are we done here?"

"You are," Gideon said. "I'll call you and schedule a meeting to wrap this up. Now get out of my sight."

Dave hurried out of the room, then Zoe turned to

Barb. "I'd like a word with Mr. Tate. Wait in the reception area and I'll drive you back to the shelter when we're finished. You and I aren't done talking."

Barb nodded and slipped out the door. Finally Zoe faced him. "How could you, Gideon?"

"How could I what? Act on information to protect my client? Stop something I knew was wrong? When you thought Barb had a lover, you should have wondered about it, too. Did you ever ask Barb if Dave really hit her?"

"No," she said, "I didn't."

"Maybe you need to start being more suspicious," he said. "Ask tougher questions."

"This has never happened before!" Zoe said hotly. "I can't think of another client where there was even a shred of doubt. And you wouldn't have known about this if I hadn't let it slip. You used our relationship to find out things about Barb."

"I didn't grill you about Barb. I didn't try to trick you," he said. "I didn't use our *relationship* to ferret out secrets about her."

"You took advantage of me," she said, snatching her file off the mahogany table and stuffing it in her briefcase.

"I followed up on the information I had. There's nothing morally or ethically wrong with that."

"Spoken like a typical lawyer."

"Exactly. Dave is my client. It's my duty to represent him as well as I can, and that's what I did."

"You didn't have to do this so publicly. You could have talked to me about it first."

"Doing something publicly works both ways, Zoe. This is a small town. A lot of people know that Barb is in your shelter and that she accused Dave of hitting her. It wasn't true, but for the rest of his life, people are going to believe he's a wife beater. He's never going to get away from that."

"What he was doing was almost as bad," Zoe said.

"*Almost* doesn't cut it," Gideon said. "Barb damaged his reputation. Forever."

"So it's okay to batter someone emotionally? Okay to call them names and ridicule them?"

"You know I'm not saying that. What Dave did was despicable. But it didn't give Barb the right to lie."

"Why didn't you tell me what you were planning?" she asked.

"And let you prepare Barb?" he answered. "The only way we were going to get the truth was by surprising her."

"I think it was because you didn't want to lose even a tiny bit of your control of the situation. You wanted to be in charge. You wanted it your way. Completely."

"Every attorney wants that."

In his professional life. But what about his private life?

What if Zoe was right? What if he was trying to control her, smothering her, instead of protecting her?

"I've got to go," she said. "Barb has some decisions to make and I want to help her."

She straightened the chairs on her side of the table, picked up the water glasses and put them on the cart that held coffee and hot water and wiped up a spill from the gleaming surface of the table.

Was she waiting for him to say something?

Before he could figure out a way to tell her how he felt, she squared her shoulders and picked up her briefcase.

"Goodbye, Gideon."

CHAPTER TWENTY-ONE

FIONA LOOKED UP from the flat of pansies she was planting in the backyard of their father's house as Zoe walked through the gate. The honeysuckle bushes along the back fence were trimmed and Fiona had dug holes in front of them for the pansies.

"Hey, Zo. How are you doing?" She brushed a bright pink lock of hair away from her face with her gloved hand, then sat back on her heels and studied her sister.

Zoe sighed. "We're going to talk about my meltdown, aren't we?"

"If you want to pretend it didn't happen, go ahead." She went back to planting the purple-and-yellow flowers.

"No." Zoe sat on the grass and let the warm breeze blow through her hair. "It was just so humiliating I don't even want to think about it."

"It's okay to lose control once in a while," Fiona said.

"Says the woman who never has," Zoe shot back. She closed her eyes. "Sorry, Fee. I didn't mean that." She tried to smile. "I'm trying to be less defensive. Clearly, I still have a lot of work to do."

"Yeah, those walls of yours are pretty high."

"Are you kidding me?" Zoe said. "*You're* talking about high walls? The woman who could give Greta 'I vant to be alone' Garbo a run for her money?"

"It's part of my mystique," Fiona said with a grin. "I'm the moody, temperamental artist, remember?"

"And I'm the solitary crusader for abused women and children," Zoe retorted. "It's taken me a long time to figure out it doesn't keep me warm at night."

Fiona glanced at her. "Thanks to Gideon, I assume?"

Zoe's throat swelled. "Yeah. Unfortunately that's over."

Her sister dropped the trowel. "What happened?"

Instead of answering, Zoe gestured at the gnarly branches of the honeysuckle. "Why don't you just dig those up? They're nothing but weeds."

"I love honeysuckle," Fiona said. "They have such a great fragrance."

"I hate them," Zoe muttered, remembering all the times she'd sat beneath the dense bushes, pretending her life was different. That she had other parents. The scent of honeysuckle blossoms brought back bad memories and childhood fears.

"I thought I was in charge of the landscaping," Fiona said.

Zoe put up her hands. "It was just a suggestion."

"Duly noted. The honeysuckle stays."

She should tell Fiona *why* she wanted to get rid of the bushes, Zoe told herself. Explain. She hesitated, unsure how Fiona would react, for her sister had shut down both her and Bree every time they'd tried to discuss their family. Then a car pulled into the driveway.

"Bree's home," Fiona said, pulling off her gardening gloves.

The opportunity to talk to Fiona about their childhood disappeared as both of them stood up to greet their sister. Zoe was relieved. And saddened.

Bree walked into the yard wearing a casual green skirt

and jacket, and carrying a briefcase. "Wow," Zoe said, forcing a smile. "You look great, Bree. Professional."

"Yeah," she said, dropping the briefcase and kicking off her heels. "I can't wait to get out of this monkey suit." She dug her toes into the grass. "The nicest day of the year so far, and I spent it with a bunch of mouthy, hormonally challenged sixteen-year-olds."

She looked at Zoe and narrowed her eyes. "Speaking of which, what are you doing here? Why aren't you at the shelter?"

Zoe almost answered truthfully. Nearly said that she couldn't focus on Safe Harbor or her job or the women there. That she was struggling with her need for control, trying to figure out how to manage it. But she hesitated too long and lost her nerve. "Are you saying I'm hormonally challenged, too?"

"If the shoe fits." Bree dropped to the grass and met Zoe's gaze. "Spill. What's going on?"

"I came to ask you guys about the furniture in the house," Zoe said, burying her real reason deep inside. "I can use whatever you don't want. A lot of the women who come through the shelter end up leaving their husbands and getting apartments. Most of them don't have a thing. They need furniture, but they can't afford it. What do you think about donating Dad's old stuff to Safe Harbor for women to use when they're starting out? We could organize it like a library. Borrow the furniture for as long as you need it, then return it so someone else can use it."

"You're asking us what we think?" Bree pretended to swoon. "I thought you had the plan all worked out. Who was in charge of what."

"Yeah, I was a little bossy. I'm sorry."

Bree shrugged. "Don't worry about it. We know how you are."

"That's the thing, Bree," Zoe said, her heart pinching. "I'm trying to change that. To delegate more. I left Sharon in charge of the shelter this afternoon. She was thrilled."

"Would Gideon have something to do with this shift in attitude?" Bree asked.

Zoe tugged at some blades of grass and stuck one in her mouth. "Why are you giving Gideon the credit?" she asked lightly. "Don't you think it's time I got a little more flexible? You've been telling me I'm too bossy my whole life." She tossed the grass away. "So. What do you think about the furniture idea?"

Bree and Fiona exchanged glances. "I think it's a great idea, Zoe," Bree said after a moment. "I like that abused women would be using Dad's things." She smiled. "Helping new families get started seems somehow to make up for what he did to us."

"That's what I thought," Zoe said. "Fee, what about you?"

"It would be great for our old furniture to be a symbol of hope, instead of the misery we endured here," Fiona said.

"Great," Zoe said briskly. "Then that's what I'll do. There's an old garage at the shelter we don't use. I'll get it cleaned out and when Bree has decided what she wants, we can move the rest of the stuff there. Once we get the furniture cleared out, we can sell the house."

She stood up to leave, but Fiona pulled her back down. "You're not going anywhere, Zo," she said. "Not until you tell us what's going on with Gideon. You were pretty slick about changing the subject, but we're not going to let you get away with it."

She could make a joke and leave, Zoe thought, or she could tell them the truth. It was put up or shut up time. If she wanted them to be open with her, she had to be open with them. She took a deep breath.

"There is no Gideon anymore. We couldn't get past the argument we had about the locks on my windows. The only time I've talked to him since that night was when we got Barb and Dave Johnson together."

"He still thinks he was right?" Bree asked, incredulous.

"He said if he couldn't protect me, he wasn't going to stick around. He wasn't going to watch someone he cared about get hurt."

He'd nearly said someone he loved. Her heart still ached from the loss.

"Bree's right. Don't back down, Zo," Fiona said. "He shouldn't have taken over like he did. And if he can't understand why you were upset, you don't have a future with him, anyway."

"The thing is, maybe I do need to be more flexible," Zoe said slowly. "I started today by leaving Sharon to handle the shelter."

"You can change yourself all you want," Fiona said. "It's not going to make any difference unless he's willing to do the same thing."

That was the question. He said he'd carried a load of guilt since Derrick died. Could he get past that? "I'm not sure it even matters." Zoe sighed. "He's from Milwaukee. He has a job there. A life. I have no idea if he's willing to let that go and move up here."

"Have you thought about moving to Milwaukee?" Fiona asked. "I'm guessing you could find a job at a shelter there pretty easily. Or open another one." She elbowed Zoe lightly in the ribs. "Use that bossiness to do good."

"Safe Harbor has been my life," Zoe said. "How can I leave it?"

Bree shrugged. "It's a building, Zoe. It's important, sure, but you're not the only one who can run it. You just said Sharon was thrilled you left her in charge. Train her to take over."

"Have you asked him to stay in Spruce Lake?" Fiona said.

"We didn't get that far," Zoe said. "For heaven's sake, we only slept together a couple of times."

"Yeah? How was it?" Fiona smiled.

"Wonderful. Earth-moving amazing. We were, ah, awake most of the night."

"You love him, don't you?" Bree said.

"Yes," Zoe said. "I love him. But I'm afraid that isn't enough."

"It's not. He has to love you, too," Fiona said. "Enough to be able to back off."

"Have either of you been in love? The forever, permanent kind of love?" Zoe asked.

"I've fallen in love once or twice," Fiona said. "Both times I took a couple of aspirin, had plenty of rest and got over it."

"Oh, Fee," Zoe said with a laugh, leaning over and giving her a hug. "One of these days you'll really fall in love."

Fiona eased away from her. "So I can be as happy as you, right?"

Zoe threw some grass at her. "What about you, Bree?"

"Yeah, I was in love. With Charlie's father. And we all know how well that turned out." She cocked her head and listened. "Speaking of Charlie, it sounds as if he's home. Do you want to stay for dinner, Zo?"

"I'd love to," she said. "But first I need to go check on how Sharon's doing at the shelter."

Fiona grinned as Charlie ambled into the backyard. "Flexibility in small doses. Right, Zo?"

ZOE CHECKED her cell phone one more time as she drove home from her sisters' later that evening. Still no message from Gideon. Maybe it really was over between them. Maybe her conversation with Bree and Fiona about what she should do didn't matter at all.

Did she want it to be over?

No!

She loved him. She needed to figure out how to make things work between them. But perhaps he didn't feel the same need.

She'd tried not to think about Gideon during the hours she'd spent with her sisters and her nephew—she'd wanted to concentrate on them. And she'd enjoyed their time together. The astonished "You're awesome, Aunt Zo" from Charlie when they'd played video games after dinner had been particularly sweet. Charlie didn't know she challenged the kids in the shelter to endless games. Sometimes it was the best way to connect with them, to get them to open up and talk.

The message light on her phone was blinking when she walked in the door, and her heart leaped. Was it Gideon?

If it was, did he want to talk to her? Or did he just want to say goodbye?

Hardly anyone called her home phone. She used her cell almost exclusively.

But what if the caller wanted to make sure the conversation was private, not public?

And if it was Gideon, maybe he just wanted to discuss Dave and Barb Johnson's case, her saner side reminded her.

Taking a deep breath, she pushed the play button, but instead of Gideon's voice, she heard nothing but the faint sound of someone breathing. She listened until the beep told her the message was over. Great. A heavy breather.

An enormous wave of disappointment crashed over her.

The next message began. "I know where you live, bitch." *Beep.*

Oh, my God. Jesse Halvorsen.

"Nice blue couch. Is it comfy? Maybe we'll find out." *Beep.*

"Wait up for me. I'm taking my wife and kid home first." *Beep.*

Zoe dropped the phone, grabbed her keys and ran out the door.

CHAPTER TWENTY-TWO

As ZOE SPED toward the shelter, she fumbled in her purse with one hand until she found her cell phone. Pushing the speed dial for 9-1-1, she spoke as soon as the dispatcher came on the line.

"Jesse Halvorsen is trying to break into Safe Harbor woman's shelter," she said, struggling to speak clearly and not shout into the phone. "He may already be inside. He's been threatening us for several days."

"Are you at the shelter, ma'am?"

"No, but he left nasty messages on the answering machine at my home." Zoe slowed as she turned a corner, then sped up again. "You need to send an officer to the shelter immediately."

"I'm contacting the police now, ma'am. Please stay on the line."

Zoe tossed the phone, still open, onto the seat next to her and gripped the steering wheel. "Are you there?" The dispatcher sounded tinny from a distance.

"I'm here," Zoe said loudly. "But I'm driving."

"Where are you going?" The dispatcher's voice rose.

"To Safe Harbor, of course."

Zoe ignored the protests from the phone as she rounded the last corner and raced toward the shelter in the next block. There was a pickup truck parked on the street in front of it, one she didn't recognize. She rolled to a stop behind it and reached for her baseball bat.

"Open the door!" a man bellowed from the front of the shelter as she jumped out of the car. Zoe heard the tinkling sound of glass breaking. "Or I'll open it myself."

"Jesse?" she called. "Is that you?"

The figure on the porch spun around. In the bright wash of light from the security system she saw an unshaven man wearing jeans and a barn coat. His dirty-blond hair looked as if it hadn't been washed in days.

"Get away from the door, Jesse. The police are on their way."

"That you, McInnes? You couldn't wait for me, huh?" he taunted. "I like a woman who's eager."

Her stomach churned at his words, and she clutched the bat in both hands. "Calm down, Jesse. This isn't doing you any good. Marilu won't want to talk to a man who's out of control."

And drunk, too, if the way he stumbled toward her was any indication.

"Marilu will talk to me anytime," he said. "You understand that?"

"We'll ask Marilu. Stay where you are, Jesse," she added as he continued to walk toward her. "Don't come any closer." Where the hell were the police? Finally she heard the roar of an engine coming closer. Thank God.

She started backing toward her car. Jesse broke into a run. She couldn't get inside the car and lock the door before he was in front of her. He reached for her, and she swung the bat. It connected with his arm with a sickening crack.

"You bitch! You broke my goddamn arm!" he yelled, staggering backward.

"And I'll break the other one if you don't get down on the ground right now."

Gideon sprinted toward her. "Get away from her!" he shouted.

"You stay out of this!" Jesse took a swing at Gideon but missed by a foot. Holding his left arm against his chest, he lurched for Gideon.

She wasn't going to let Jesse try to hit Gideon again. "Down on the ground, Jesse." She raised the bat as if ready to hit a fastball. Jesse stared at her for a moment, then dropped to his knees. "All the way."

He grunted with pain as he awkwardly lay down. When he was completely prone, Zoe leaned against the car. The bat dropped out of her hands and rolled under the vehicle.

"My God, Zoe." Gideon reached for her, holding her shoulders as he examined her. "Are you hurt?"

"I'm fine, Gideon." She wrapped her arms around him and held on tightly. "What are you doing here?"

"I've been trying to find you," he said, clutching her equally hard. "I called the shelter, and while I was talking to Sharon, someone started pounding on the shelter's front door. I told her to call the police, then I came over." He pressed her head against his chest and she felt his mouth move on her hair. "God! I saw you confronting him, but I was too far away to do anything about it."

Jesse stirred, and Gideon snatched the bat from beneath the car. "Don't move or I'll break your skull, you worthless piece of trash," he growled.

They heard a siren in the distance. Flashing lights turned onto the shelter's street, and a few moments later a police officer jumped out of the car. It was Bobby Jasper, one of the younger officers.

"What seems to be the problem?" he said.

Gideon gestured to Jesse. "He was trying to break into the shelter and he assaulted Ms. McInnes."

Bobby grabbed Jesse by the collar and hauled him to his feet, patting him down as he spoke. "You drunk and stupid again, Halvorsen?"

"He went way beyond stupid," Zoe said. "He broke a window in the shelter. And he was coming after me."

"She busted my arm!" Jesse whined.

"You're lucky that's all she did," Bobby said.

"She was protecting herself," Gideon said. "I saw the whole thing, but I was too far away to help her."

"I believe you, Zoe." Bobby gave her a level look. "Chief Dobbs doesn't speak for the rest of the force." He prodded Jesse toward the squad car. "Let me secure him, then you can answer a few questions."

Bobby took her statement and Gideon's, then spoke to Sharon in the shelter. A few minutes later he came out. "I'll drive Halvorsen to the hospital, then book him for assault, breaking and entering, disturbing the peace and whatever else I can think of. And I'll have patrol keep an eye on your house tonight."

"Thanks, Bobby."

The police officer nodded, then walked back to his vehicle.

Zoe watched until the squad car drove away. Then she said, "I'm sorry you had to see that." Gideon was no doubt beating himself up because he'd gotten there too late to protect her.

"Zoe…" he began, but she put her hand on his arm.

"Not now, Gideon. I have to make sure everyone in the shelter is all right."

The broken window was the only physical damage

But everyone had heard Jesse shouting. The women huddled at the bottom of the stairs with Sharon. Some of them had children clinging to their legs. They all looked shell-shocked.

"You want me to look after the kids?" Gideon murmured.

"That would be great," she said.

She watched as he got on the floor and said something to the four girls and three boys. They all nodded, then Gideon stood up.

"If we're going to make popcorn, someone's going to have to show me where the kitchen is," he said.

"I will!" one of the girls piped up.

"No, me!"

"It's this way." The smallest boy danced in front of Gideon, pointing to the back of the house.

All of them disappeared into the other room, and Zoe turned to a blond woman who was crying. Her daughter was one of the children who'd gone with Gideon. "Marilu, are you all right?"

Marilu sniffled. "He's gone, hasn't he?"

"Yes," Zoe said. "He's on his way to jail."

"Did he hurt you?" Marilu asked fearfully.

"No, he didn't." Zoe put her arm around Marilu's shoulders and led her into the living room, and the other women trailed behind. "Anyone want to talk about what just happened?" she asked.

Nobody said anything, and Zoe sank onto the couch. They'd discuss it in their group session the next day, after everyone had processed the confrontation. Tonight, she'd stay until they'd all calmed down. "I'm too wound up to go home," she said. "Anyone want to watch some TV?"

An hour later she and Gideon left the shelter. All the

children were asleep, and their mothers had gone to bed, as well. Sharon, although shaken, said she was fine and didn't need Zoe to stay. Gideon had nailed a piece of wood over the broken window.

"Will you come home with me, Gideon?" Zoe said. The night was cool, but the air was fragrant with the smell of blooming plants. New life.

"You think you could keep me away?" he said, his arm tight around her shoulders.

She leaned into him as they walked to her car. Once she was inside, he said, "I'll follow you home."

Her front door was ajar when she stepped onto the porch, and uneasiness washed over her. Gideon got out of his car and bounded up the steps, and she gestured to the open door. "I'm pretty sure I left it like that. But it's freaking me out."

Instead of the lecture she expected, he dropped a kiss on her head. "Stay out here while I check the house."

A couple minutes later he waved her in. "Everything is fine."

Tossing her jacket on a chair, she moved to the couch and sat. "Thank goodness you were here, Gideon."

"Glad to provide house-searching services." He stood by the now closed front door. Was he upset with her for leaving the door open? Or with himself because he thought he'd failed to protect her against Jesse?

"I meant at the shelter." She stood up and crossed to him. "I'm glad you were at Safe Harbor tonight. And that I didn't have to face Jesse by myself."

"You did just fine," he said, tucking a strand of hair behind her ear. "You had the situation under control."

She stroked his cheek. "And you're beating yourself up about it, aren't you?"

He pulled her into his arms and buried his face in her hair. "It was my worst nightmare come to life," he said, his voice muffled. "Everything I was most afraid of." He held her close for a moment, then eased away. "I knew I couldn't get to you before he did. I had to watch him run at you and I couldn't do anything to stop him."

"I know," she said, her arms tightening around his neck. "I finally understand. When Jesse tried to punch you, I wanted to swing that baseball bat at his head and crack it open like an egg. I would have, too, if he hadn't gotten on the ground."

A little warmth returned to his dark gaze. "You were an Amazon, Zoe. He wasn't drunk enough to ignore that. I would have backed down, too."

"I was angry at you yesterday because I thought you were trying to control me," she said softly. "Trying to tell me what to do, take away my power. I didn't understand what you were feeling.

"Now I do. Now I realize how I would have reacted if our positions had been reversed. I would have wanted to step between you and danger. I would have tried anything to protect you."

"But screwdrivers wouldn't have been involved, right?" he said, the glimmer of a smile on his mouth.

"I would have asked you first if it had been *your* windows. But I understand now that you fixed the latches for the right reasons." She held her breath, hoping he understood her position, as well.

"Can we sit down, Zoe?" he said.

Her budding happiness vanished, replaced by uncertainty. Would he tell her he couldn't live with the risks she took? Would he say it had been too hard for him tonight, and he didn't want to go through this again?

He sat close to her on the couch and took her hand. "I transferred my father to a rehabilitation center in Green Bay today. That's why I didn't call you earlier. I drove there behind the ambulance and made sure he was settled into his room. I spent a lot of time talking to the doctors and the therapists." He shoved a hand through his hair. "I even had dinner with him."

"That was very generous, Gideon." Especially considering how Gideon felt about his father. She laced her fingers through his, thrilled when he squeezed her hand.

"No, it wasn't generous. I did it to assuage my guilt. I resented having to deal with him, make all the arrangements, when I knew he'd just be angry at me for doing it. You shouldn't begrudge taking care of your parents."

"Of course you resented him," Zoe said. "He discarded you when you were a child, but you had to put your own life on hold to come here and take care of him. I think most people would have felt the same way."

"I had a lot of time to think today," he said. "I was angry at you when I found out you were with Wallace when he had his stroke."

"There's a news flash," she murmured.

He pulled her closer. "I wanted to blame you, just like I blamed you for Derrick's death. I'd failed to protect him. I told myself that if I'd kept in touch with my brother, if I'd tried to have a relationship with him, I might have been able to save him from you."

"You couldn't save him from himself," she said. "No one could have done that."

"I didn't want to admit that. It made me completely powerless. My brother died because I couldn't do anything to help him. I swore I'd never feel that way again."

"Then Jesse tried to throw a brick through my window, and you felt powerless a second time," she said softly. "You weren't able to catch him."

"And I overreacted and rode roughshod over you," he admitted. "But I *had* to protect you. I wasn't going to let another person I loved get hurt. Or worse."

Her heart turned over in her chest. "What?"

"I got it, Zoe. I realized what I'd done. I took your power away, and that was the last thing I wanted to do."

"Forget about my power for a minute," she said, wrapping her arms around his neck. "I want to know if you meant what you said."

"Every word."

"Really?"

"Yes, Zoe. I got it. You were right and I was wrong," he said, but his eyes were twinkling.

Her heart fluttered against her ribs. "Not that, you infuriating man. The other thing you said."

He pulled her into his lap. "You mean the part about loving you?"

"Yes," she said, holding her breath. She needed to hear the words.

"Of course I love you," he said, cupping her face in his hands. "Why do you think I acted like such an idiot?"

"I love you, too, Gideon," she said, her heart expanding. "So much it scares me. I was afraid I'd pushed you away. That you were going to leave Spruce Lake and never look back."

"Are you kidding me?" he said, brushing his mouth over hers. "I was plotting how to get you back. I couldn't walk away from you."

"And I wasn't going to let you," she said. "You have me, and I'm never letting you go."

"Promise?"

"What will it take to convince you?"

He shifted beneath her, and she felt his erection against her legs. "Hmm. Let me think."

Happiness bubbled through her in a heady rush. "While you're trying to decide, do you mind if I take off my sweater? It's getting a little warm in here."

"Of course not. I'd hate for you to get overheated."

"Really?" She paused with her top half-off. "Because I'd counted on getting overheated. More than once tonight."

"Yeah?" He smoothed his hands over her abdomen, lingered at her waist. "More than once?"

"Several times."

She tossed the sweater to the floor and unhooked her bra. His gaze intensified as she let it drop from her arms. "You're starting to convince me."

Without moving off his lap, she managed to pull off her jeans and thong. Then she yanked his T-shirt over his head. "You're falling behind," she said breathlessly.

"Not a chance," he said, standing up with her in his arms. He headed for the bedroom. "Let's go discuss this in more detail."

"I like details," she said, kissing him.

AN HOUR LATER, he lifted himself onto his elbow beside her on the bed. "Marry me, Zoe."

"I thought you'd never ask." She twined her legs around his.

"You distracted me and made me lose my train of thought," he said.

"Poor baby," she murmured, stroking him. "Do you think I could do it again?"

He captured her hand and brought it to his mouth.

"Not until you've answered my question. Will you marry me, Zoe?"

"Yes, Gideon." Happiness bubbled like champagne in her veins. "I never thought I'd say this again, but I want to marry you. I want to spend my life with you. I want to laugh with you, fight with you, have children with you. Grow old with you."

"You want to do it soon, I hope," he said, drawing his finger down her nose. "I'm not going to give you a chance to change your mind."

"Not going to happen," she said, sitting up and drawing the sheet over her chest. "But you'll have to wait long enough for Fiona to make rings for us."

"Works for me," he said, rolling onto his back so that she ended up on top of him. "It will take me a while to put my condo up for sale and give notice at work. But I don't want to wait a day longer than we have to."

"You're going to move to Spruce Lake?" she asked, her joy expanding until it filled every corner of her heart.

"Of course I am. Your shelter is here. All the women you've helped, all the contacts you've built. Bree and Charlie are here. All I have in Milwaukee is a job. I can set up my own practice or work for the DA's office. I'll figure out what I want to do. The only absolute is it has to be here. With you."

She threw her arms around his neck. "We'll replace all the sad memories of Spruce Lake with happy ones, Gideon. We'll make a family here, you and I. A home."

"I like the sound of that," he said, holding her close. "Spruce Lake. A place called home."

* * * * *

*Be sure to read the other two
McKinnes triplets' stories—
Bree's in December 2008,
and Fiona's in 2009.*

The Colton family is back!
Enjoy a sneak preview of
COLTON'S SECRET SERVICE
by Marie Ferrarella,
part of
THE COLTONS: FAMILY FIRST
miniseries.

Available from Silhouette Romantic Suspense
in September 2008.

He cautioned himself to be leery. He was human and he'd been conned before. But never by anyone nearly so attractive. Never by anyone he'd felt so attracted to.

In her defense, Nick supposed that Georgie could actually be telling him the truth. That she was a victim in all this. He had his people back in California checking her out, to make sure she was who she said she was and had, as she claimed, not even been near a computer but on the road these last few months that the threats had been made.

In the meantime, he was doing his own checking out. Up close and exceedingly personal. So personal he could feel his blood stirring.

It had been a long time since he'd thought of himself as anything other than a law enforcement agent of one type or other. But Georgeann Grady made him remember that beneath the oaths he had taken and his devotion to duty, there beat the heart of a man.

A man who'd been far too long without the touch of a woman.

He watched as the light from the fireplace caressed the outline of Georgie's small, trim, jean-clad body as she moved about the rustic living room that could have easily come off the set of a Hollywood Western. Except that it was genuine.

As genuine as she claimed to be?

Something inside of him hoped so.

He wasn't supposed to be taking sides. His only interest in being here was to guarantee Senator Joe Colton's safety as the latter continued to make his bid for the presidency. Everything else was supposed to be secondary, but, Nick had to silently admit, that was just a wee bit hard to remember right now.

Earlier, before she'd put her precocious handful of a daughter to bed, Georgie had fed his appetite by whipping up some kind of a delicious concoction out of the vegetables she'd pulled from her garden. Vegetables that, by all rights, should have been withered and dried. She'd mentioned that a friend came by on occasion to weed and tend it. Still, it surprised him that somehow she'd managed to make something mouthwatering out of it.

Almost as mouthwatering as she looked to him right at this moment.

Again, he was reminded of the appetite that hadn't been fed, hadn't been satisfied.

And wasn't going to be, Nick sternly told himself. At least not now. Maybe later, when things took on a more definite shape and all the questions in his head were answered to his satisfaction, there would be time to explore this feeling. This woman. But not now.

Damn it.

"Sorry about the lack of light," Georgie said, breaking into his train of thought as she turned around to face him. If she noticed the way he was looking at her, she gave no indication. "But I don't see a point in paying for electricity if I'm not going to be here. Besides, Emmie really enjoys camping out. She likes roughing it."

"And you?" Nick asked, moving closer to her, so close that a whisper would have trouble fitting in. "What do you like?"

The very breath stopped in Georgie's throat as she looked up at him.

"I think you've got a fair shot of guessing that one," she told him softly.

* * * * *

Be sure to look for COLTON'S SECRET SERVICE
and the other following titles from
THE COLTONS: FAMILY FIRST *miniseries:*
RANCHER'S REDEMPTION
by Beth Cornelison
THE SHERIFF'S AMNESIAC BRIDE
by Linda Conrad
SOLDIER'S SECRET CHILD
by Caridad Piñeiro
BABY'S WATCH
by Justine Davis
A HERO OF HER OWN
by Carla Cassidy

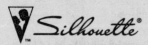

Silhouette®

Romantic
SUSPENSE

Sparked by Danger,
Fueled by Passion.

The Coltons Are Back!

Marie Ferrarella
Colton's Secret Service

The Coltons: Family First

On a mission to protect a senator, Secret Service agent
Nick Sheffield tracks down a threatening message only
to discover Georgie Gradie Colton, a rodeo-riding single
mom, who insists on her innocence. Nick is instantly
taken with the feisty redhead, but vows not to let his
feelings interfere with his mission. Now he must figure
out if this woman is conning him or if he can trust her
and the passion they share....

Available September wherever books are sold.

**Look for upcoming Colton titles
from Silhouette Romantic Suspense:**
RANCHER'S REDEMPTION by Beth Cornelison, Available October
THE SHERIFF'S AMNESIAC BRIDE by Linda Conrad, Available November
SOLDIER'S SECRET CHILD by Caridad Piñeiro, Available December
BABY'S WATCH by Justine Davis, Available January 2009
A HERO OF HER OWN by Carla Cassidy, Available February 2009

SAVE $1.00

A riveting trilogy from
BRENDA NOVAK

SAVE $1.00 on the purchase price of one book in The Last Stand trilogy from Brenda Novak.

Offer valid from May 27, 2008, to August 30, 2008.
Redeemable at participating retail outlets. Limit one coupon per purchase.

52608328

5 65373 00076 2   (8100) 0 11499

MBNTRI08CPN

REQUEST YOUR FREE BOOKS!

2 FREE NOVELS PLUS 2 FREE GIFTS!

HARLEQUIN®

Super Romance®

Exciting, emotional, unexpected!

YES! Please send me 2 FREE Harlequin Superromance® novels and my 2 FREE gifts (gifts are worth about $10). After receiving them, if I don't wish to receive any more books, I can return the shipping statement marked "cancel." If I don't cancel, I will receive 6 brand-new novels every month and be billed just $4.69 per book in the U.S. or $5.24 per book in Canada, plus 25¢ shipping and handling per book and applicable taxes, if any*. That's a savings of close to 15% off the cover price! I understand that accepting the 2 free books and gifts places me under no obligation to buy anything. I can always return a shipment and cancel at any time. Even if I never buy another book from Harlequin, the two free books and gifts are mine to keep forever.

135 HDN EEX7   336 HDN EEYK

Name	(PLEASE PRINT)	
Address		Apt. #
City	State/Prov.	Zip/Postal Code

Signature (if under 18, a parent or guardian must sign)

Mail to the **Harlequin Reader Service:**
IN U.S.A.: P.O. Box 1867, Buffalo, NY 14240-1867
IN CANADA: P.O. Box 609, Fort Erie, Ontario L2A 5X3

Not valid to current subscribers of Harlequin Superromance books.

Want to try two free books from another line?
Call 1-800-873-8635 or visit www.morefreebooks.com.

* Terms and prices subject to change without notice. N.Y. residents add applicable sales tax. Canadian residents will be charged applicable provincial taxes and GST. Offer not valid in Quebec. This offer is limited to one order per household. All orders subject to approval. Credit or debit balances in a customer's account(s) may be offset by any other outstanding balance owed by or to the customer. Please allow 4 to 6 weeks for delivery. Offer available while quantities last.

Your Privacy: Harlequin is committed to protecting your privacy. Our Privacy Policy is available online at www.eHarlequin.com or upon request from the Reader Service. From time to time we make our lists of customers available to reputable third parties who may have a product or service of interest to you. If you would prefer we not share your name and address, please check here. ☐

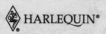

HARLEQUIN Super Romance

COMING NEXT MONTH

#1512 TO SAVE A FAMILY • Anna DeStefano
Atlanta Heroes

Public defender Emma Montgomery fights for the underdog, and that usually means butting heads with Lieutenant Rick Downing. When their latest skirmish involves a single mother with three kids, Emma is determined to see justice done. But falling for Rick wasn't part of the plan....

#1513 AN IMPERFECT MATCH • Kimberly Van Meter
You, Me & the Kids

What is Dean Halvorsen supposed to do when Annabelle Nichols shows up at his construction office needing a job? Turn her down? Not likely, especially after he sees her baby girl, Honey. The trouble is the single dad is having a hard time keeping his distance from the gorgeous single mom!

#1514 HER FAVORITE HUSBAND • Caron Todd

Falling in love is easy for Sarah Bretton. Staying in love's the trick. Two failed marriages later, Sarah has tracked down Ian Kingsley, her first ex, in northern Canada, the so-called land of the midnight sun. And now the fun begins....

#1515 A FATHER FOR DANNY • Janice Carter
Suddenly a Parent

Samantha Sorrenti is in the business of finding things. But this is the first time anyone's hired her to find some*one*. And at twelve years old, Danny is her youngest client ever. With the help of her twin sister, she tracks down Chase Sullivan and complicates his already complicated life with the news he has a son. A son who needs him desperately.

#1516 HIS BROTHER'S SECRET • Debra Salonen
Spotlight on Sentinel Pass

He thought he could arrive in town, make amends, then leave. But when Shane Reynard sees Jenna Murphy again, his past longing for her is resurrected. Still, he has to confess what his twin did to her. And that could end this relationship before it even starts.

#1517 STRANGER AT THE DOOR • Laura Abbot
Everlasting Love

Eloping with air force pilot Sam Lambert had not been in Isabel Lambert's plans. But through the years she and Sam built a good life. Then it all changed with the appearance of a man claiming to be Sam's son. Could they move beyond Sam's past
and stay together?

HSRCNM0808